"I wouldn't do that, Kane."

Blessed leveled the pistol, stopping the charging Kane in his tracks.

Kane said, "It's you who should die, Blessed. You're a scoundrel. You're responsible for the death of my mother, and that alone makes you worthy of death."

Blessed snickered. "But instead I'll have riches. Nice irony, eh? It's the way of the world, Kane, and I . . ." He stopped. Kane's gaze bored into him like fire.

"What are you looking at?" he demanded.

"I'm looking at a liar, and a murderer, and nothing more," Kane said.

Blessed laughed coldly. "I ought to kill you right here. . . . Hell, why not?"

In one motion he cocked the pistol, aimed at Kane's face, and fired.

HUNTER'S JOURNEY

Judson Gray

A SIGNET BOOK

SIGNET
Published by New American Library, a division of
Penguin Putnam Inc., 375 Hudson Street,
New York, New York 10014, U.S.A.
Penguin Books Ltd, 27 Wrights Lane,
London W8 5TZ, England
Penguin Books Australia Ltd, Ringwood,
Victoria, Australia
Penguin Books Canada Ltd, 10 Alcorn Avenue,
Toronto, Ontario, Canada M4V 3B2
Penguin Books (N.Z.) Ltd, 182–190 Wairau Road,
Auckland 10, New Zealand

Penguin Books Ltd, Registered Offices:
Harmondsworth, Middlesex, England

First published by Signet, an imprint of New American Library,
a division of Penguin Putnam Inc.

First Printing, August 1999
10 9 8 7 6 5 4 3 2 1

Preface

His name is Kanati Porterfell, and he is on the run, both as the hunter and as the hunted.

The son of a Cherokee mother he loved dearly and a white father he has never known, Kane carries in his memory the contents of several secret, encoded letters, pieces of a puzzle that purports to lead to a treasure of unsurpassed value—the legendary Punjab Star diamond, said to have been lost years before in a violent Civil War incident that involved William Porterfell, the father Kane until recently thought was long dead.

Only one final piece of the puzzle does Kane not possess: the contents of the last coded letter, existing now only in the mind of William Porterfell. Only when father and son come together, to re-create the letters and break the code, will there be any hope that the diamond can be found.

Kane, kidnapped by the ruthless Robert Blessed, an old wartime associate of William Porterfell who will stop at nothing to gain the jewel and restore his own faded wealth, has escaped and now flees across the American West in the final days of 1885, seeking his father while trying to evade Robert Blessed . . . if Blessed is still alive. When Kane left Colorado, that question remained unanswered.

But Kane has been in this situation before, and he knows it is unsafe to assume anything other than that Blessed still lives and is as dangerous as ever.

During his quest Kane has seen the best and the worst of the frontier, has been helped by some and hurt by many. But good has also come with the bad, and the best of it is Carolina Railey, the half-Cherokee daughter of a stage magician who has befriended Kane.

In a strike-torn Colorado mining town, Kane almost found his father and almost lost his life. Now he presses on, following his strongest lead yet toward Helena, in the Montana Territory. A new year is about to dawn, filling Kane with hope and trepidation, and danger still follows close behind.

In Helena Kane hopes to find his father at last and come to the end of his journey.

But for now, the chase goes on, full of danger, full of adventure.

Chapter 1

He took a few more steps through the snow and realized that, somehow, he seemed to be floating instead of walking. Kanati Porterfell marveled over this miraculous development—until he pitched forward into the snow and realized the truth. He'd not been floating. He'd simply grown unable to feel his feet. They were numb, nerveless, overcome by the cold.

He sent up a fervent prayer: *Don't let me lose my feet. Please, whatever happens, God, don't let me lose my feet.*

He pushed himself upright again. Pain shot up his ankles. Though the excruciating stab made him cry out, he was grateful for the pain. Pain proved he was still alive and that his body wasn't ruined. Not yet.

He plunged on, then paused to catch his breath. The air burned his lungs like a cold iron. He lifted his hat, touched his head, and looked at his frigid fingers. Crusted blood flecked off his flesh like rust.

"My name is Kane Porterfell," he said loudly, just so he'd not forget, as he already had a time or two during this endless journey. He'd stopped and looked around him at the empty white Montana landscape and found he could not recall why he was here, where he was going, even who he was.

He went forward again with that same detached, floating sensation, unable to feel his feet beneath him. Once, as a child, he'd seen the black, twisted feet of a man who had suffered severe frostbite. The sight had horrified him. He'd dreamed for years afterward about those gnarled, sooty, dried-grapevine toes.

So he prayed again, a whispered internal chant: *Don't let me lose my toes, don't let me lose my feet, don't let me lose my toes, don't let me lose my feet . . .*

On he pushed through the driving snow.

His mind began to go blank on him again, and he fought it with a silent recitation. *I am Kanati Porterfell. Half white, half Cherokee. Born in the mountains of North Carolina, among the Cherokee remnant there.* He forced his mind to picture those mountains, lush and foggy and green.

And warm in the summer. So different from this killing cold.

He trudged forward, fighting the impulse to yield to the frigid chill, because to yield would be to die.

He continued his mental recitation. Born in North Carolina . . . but moved, later, to the Nations. Other Cherokees, the children of the Trail of Tears, were there. He had become one of them, raised by his Cherokee mother. His white father—what was his name? William Porterfell?—was absent, thought dead.

But Bill Porterfell wasn't dead. Kane knew that

now and sought to find him here in this icy wasteland.

He squinted against the cold wind. His thoughts darted back and forth, out of control and hard to catch, like the water spiders that skittered across the surface of the cool Carolina mountain pools of his childhood days.

Kane touched his head again. Pain shot through his temples. With concern, he realized that he couldn't remember how he'd been hurt. Why couldn't he remember? Was it the injury itself? Maybe it was the biting cold.

Or maybe he was dying out here, his mind failing first.

Memories rushed back. *A robbery.* A train on which he'd been riding toward the western mountains had been stopped in the midst of the snowstorm, the tracks blocked by fallen timber. Men with weapons had herded the passengers out. They'd stripped necklaces and bracelets from the women, watches and money from the men. Meanwhile, other robbers had looted the baggage car.

They hadn't robbed Kane. Kane knew why they'd avoided him. He'd seen it in the eyes of the robber who had passed him by. A look of loathing, as though Kane bore a gruesome disease.

He understood: He hadn't been robbed simply because he was Cherokee. The robber hadn't wanted to touch an Indian. Other than Kane's pistol, the man had taken nothing from him.

Too bad for the robber, Kane thought. He had several hundred dollars hidden inside the lining of his coat.

He staggered further, wondering where he was going, if anywhere. He fell again and struggled to rise. This time it took longer.

His mind threatened to fade on him again, but he forced it back to the robbery, making himself recall every detail, just to exercise his faltering brain.

Something had happened . . . something had gone wrong and sparked violence. But what? He thought hard and finally remembered.

A young man, somewhat dandified and obviously insulted at being robbed, had thrown something on one of the robbers. Something stinking and offensive . . .

Urine! Kane had been almost as shocked as the robber who'd been baptized by the stuff. The young man had been wearing one of those long tubes designed to strap to the leg beneath the trousers, a discreet receptacle often used by male travelers on long train trips. He had managed to unfasten the thing, pull it free, and use its contents as a weapon of insult.

It was a foolish thing for him to do. The sodden train robber, aided by another, had attacked the fellow and might have beaten him to death had not Kane and two other men intervened. Quite a struggle that had been! Somewhere in the midst of it, Kane had received a blow on the head that knocked him senseless.

He'd come to alone, far away from the tracks, out in the snow. The train was gone. Kane knew what they'd done. To punish the impudent Indian for daring to attack them, the robbers had ridden him far away, out onto the plains for many miles, and dumped him off into the snow.

He'd been left to die.

But he wouldn't die. Not without a fight.

There were trees ahead; probably a streamside grove. But Kane was growing very weak. His head throbbed. He wondered if he had other injuries he hadn't detected yet. He felt sick and feverish.

He struggled toward the trees, praying for strength.

Closer. Almost there. Maybe among the trees he would find some shelter from the snow. But still the cold would be there, the kind of cold that flowed around and through a person as if it were liquid through a sieve.

Kane reached the trees and pulled himself among them. A creek flowed through the copse. He knelt beside it to drink but found it frozen. He rammed the ice with his hand to break the surface, then he drank deeply and used a handful of water to gently wash his wounded head.

He felt so astonishingly tired. The idea of sleep was irresistible. He would lie down here and rest for just a few moments. Not long enough to let himself freeze to death. Just a few moments.

He sank into the snow and closed his eyes.

Pain rippled through him. He groaned, gritting his teeth, and tried to open his eyes. He couldn't.

The pain intensified. Then he sensed something strange . . . he was conscious of being touched. Rubbed. He tried again to pry open his eyes, this time succeeding just enough to let in light and a few jumbled, shifting images. He moaned again, closing his eyes.

"Coming around, are you? Good. Good. You'll be well now. I got to you quick enough."

It was a man's voice. Kane struggled to move, and his teeth began to chatter. The air around him was warm, but still he was cold . . . cold in a deep-inside, permeating way, as if his very core had been chilled too deeply to ever thaw.

"The name's Spence," the man's voice said from somewhere in the world beyond his closed eyelids. "Got that name because my last name is Spencer. But it ain't really Spencer no more. Just Spence. One name serves for all purposes. Easier that way."

Kane forced his eyelids apart. This time he was able to discern a white fellow, burly and plain-faced, leaning across him and gingerly rubbing his left arm with calloused hands. Kane held his blurred gaze on the man a few moments longer, wondering what the devil was going on. Then he understood. The man was trying to restore circulation and warmth to his nearly frozen body.

"Got your eyes open now, do you? Good! I reckon you're going to make it. And believe it or not, young man, I don't even think you're going to lose no toes. Mighty close, though, mighty close. If I had found you five, ten minutes later than I did, I don't think you'd have had nary a chance to keep them. Hell, you'd probably have froze to death."

Kane felt he should speak to this man, but he

didn't seem to know how to go about it anymore. He managed to move his lips slowly, but no words came out.

"You took a knock on the noggin, young man," Spence said, moving now to Kane's other arm and rubbing it just as gingerly. The pain Kane felt as blood and heat returned to him was quite fierce. "How in the devil you managed to wind up lying in the snow beside a creek, way out here in the rump country of godforsook Egypt, with your head busted, is something I ain't quite figured out yet. But you'll tell me, I reckon, when you can. Right? Right!" He chuckled, and Kane was struck by something unusual in this man's manner: He was talking too fast, too much, and seemed nervous.

Kane closed his eyes again and tried to relax, though the cold that held his innards in its grip, combined with the sharp, tingling pains that Spence's ministrations to his arms were generating, kept him from it.

But he must have slept, or perhaps passed out, because when he opened his eyes again, everything looked different. The light was more dim, now golden and flickering. The air was colder around him . . . but he himself felt warmer. Though he was lying down, he felt quite dizzy, like he was in a spinning, tilting room.

Spence was beside him, leaning over, his face close and grinning. "Well! Awake again, are you? I was beginning to think you weren't going to join me again."

Kane's lips were dry, his throat as well. He tried to clear it.

"Water? That what you need?" Spence sprang up and moved out of Kane's range of vision for a few moments. He returned with a dipper of water. Helping Kane hold his head up a little, he held the ladle and allowed Kane to drink slowly. He'd never had a more satisfying, healing drink than this one.

Kane's head sank back into the straw-stuffed mattress. "Thank you," he whispered.

"Talking again, too! Hey, you an Indian?"

"Part . . . Cherokee."

"Yeah. I thought so. You look it."

"How did I get here?"

"I carried you! Like a sack of meal. You wouldn't have lived much longer if I hadn't found you." Spence's face came close again, and he flashed a dirty-toothed grin. "I reckon you might say you owe me your life."

"Thank . . . you."

"You hungry?"

"No . . . I don't think so. More water, though."

Spence complied. Kane drank again, but this time with an uncomfortable feeling, because Spence was hanging his homely face too close to his, and grinning oddly, his brown eyes flickering in the dim and wavering light of the fireplace in this low-roofed place. Even when Kane had drained the dipper, Spence remained where he was, staring deeply at him, with an expression Kane could only think of as animalistically cunning.

"So . . . your name's Kane, is it?"

"Yes . . . how did you know?"

"You been talking, young man. While you was lying there, all senseless, you still was talking. Why, you was rambling right on when I found you lying out in the snow. I figured out your name from it all." He paused, still grinning. "A lot of what you said, I couldn't make much sense of. Just a lot of babble. But some of it came through clear as a Sunday sermon."

Kane shrugged away from Spence's looming visage. He felt sick and hot. His head ached. "I think maybe I am hungry, after all." He wasn't, but he had to find some way to make Spence move away.

Spence nodded. "All righty. I'll get you some food. Biscuits and beef suit you?"

"Yes."

The intensity of Spence's glare suddenly heightened. His tongue swept out across his lips almost lizardlike. "So . . . tell me, Kane. Where's the treasure?"

"Treasure . . ."

"That's right. Come on, tell me! I'm the man who saved you from freezing to death. I just want to know what it is, that's all. Just curious, you know."

Kane said, "I don't know about any treasure."

"Sure you do. I heard you talking on and on about it. You even said what it was. So you may as well tell old Spence all about the Punjab Star."

Kane knew then that he had indeed been talking. If he'd gone so far as to reveal that the lost treasure was the Punjab Star diamond, he'd said a great deal too much.

"I must have been out of my head," Kane said in

a tired, grating voice. "I don't know about any treasure."

Spence, only half-grinning now, stared at Kane in silence, then said, "I'll get them victuals for you."

Chapter 2

Spence stood and walked across the room toward the fireplace. Kane pushed himself up a little and looked around, though the effort made his injured head throb and let him know just how sick he was. He was inside a small cabin. Outside, the wind howled, and cold leaked through the log walls here and there, but all in all the place was reasonably warm. Or maybe it was just the fire of fever that warmed him.

He would ask Spence what kind of place this was later. For now, he felt too sick to talk.

He only wished he hadn't talked so much already. How much had he said about the treasure, and his quest? And how much of the aid Spence was giving him was inspired by human kindness and how much, maybe, by the hope that Kane could lead him to something of value?

He closed his eyes and rested some more but didn't let himself fall asleep. The smell of baking biscuits soon filled the little cabin, making him painfully aware of the emptiness of his belly.

When Spence came to him with a cracked plate

laden with cold beef and hot biscuits, Kane noticed that he had a knife in his hand as well.

"Here you go." Spence handed the plate down to Kane, but kept the knife.

Kane took the plate. Spence was staring at him thoughtfully, not quite grinning. That cunning look and manner were all the more noticeable now—and unsettling.

"You going to eat or not?"

Kane shuffled himself to a seated position, fought dizziness for a moment, then said, "I'll eat."

He took a bite of biscuit, his eyes fixed on the knife in Spence's hand. Spence noticed, and raised the knife slightly. "I want you to give some thought to that treasure I asked you about," he said. "Maybe you'll remember something about it." Suddenly the knife came forward, almost into Kane's face. A tense, silent moment held.

"You'll be wanting this to cut the meat, I reckon," Spence said. He flipped the knife before Kane's eyes and caught it by the blade, holding the handle out to Kane.

Kane took it. "Thank you."

"Don't mention it."

Spence turned and walked back to the rough, low fireplace, where he knelt and extended his hands, warming them against the fire's glow. Kane ate silently and stared at Spence's dark form outlined against the firelight.

Kane hoped he wasn't hurt as badly as he feared, because he wanted to heal up and get away from here and this troubling man.

At least Spence made good biscuits, though it took all of Kane's energy just to chew and swallow them.

Kane was finishing his final bite when Spence rose suddenly and turned. He had a pistol in his hand.

Kane said, "What are you—"

"Hush!" Spence said, raising his free hand. "Listen! You hear it?"

Kane heard nothing but the crackling of the fire and the howling of the wind outside.

"Somebody's coming," Spence said. "There's somebody out there. He's calling out . . . did you hear?"

Kane still heard nothing; he was beginning to wonder if he'd wound up in a cabin with a madman who heard phantom voices in the howling wind. Kane set the plate aside . . . but kept the knife in hand, beneath the dirty blanket that covered him.

For half a minute Spence stood tensely, head cocked, pistol in hand, and Kane wondered who it was that this man feared, and why.

Something, or someone, hammered hard on the door. It was so loud and unexpected that Kane almost leaped out of the bed.

Spence backed two steps toward the fire, raised pistol toward the door, and thumbed back the hammer.

The pounding on the door came again.

"Spence!" a husky voice called. "Spence, let me in . . . let me in . . ."

Spence muttered a curse, thumbed down the hammer of his pistol and stuck the weapon under his belt. He went to the door and opened it. Snow swirled in. Cold air struck Kane like a slap and made his muscles tense. His head throbbed and he felt a surge of sickness.

"Lord's sake, Martin, what the devil's happened to you?" Spence said to the man who stood in the doorway, hunched over and trembling. "Get inside!"

The man staggered in. That he was hurt was obvious. His face was pallid, like a corpse's, and he held his hands tightly to his side. Kane saw blood on his fingers.

"I'm hurt, Spence," Martin said. "Got to lie down."

The man turned and stumbled toward the bunk on which Kane lay. He stopped when he saw Kane. "Who the deuce . . ."

"It's a hurt redskin fellow," Spence said. "Go lie down on my bunk, Martin."

The man, eyes red from the cold and squinting from the pain he was obviously in, gazed at Kane a couple of moments, puzzled. As Kane looked back at him, the man's image wavered. A new wave of nausea swept over Kane. His head felt like it was coming apart. He closed his eyes, groaning softly.

He opened them again when he heard a heavy thud. Martin, apparently almost as bad off as he, had collapsed, legs folding up beneath him, and now sat precariously on the floor. Spence came over and began to pull at him, trying to get him on his feet again.

"Leave me be!" Martin said sharply, waving him off. "I can get up myself. Keep your Judas hands off me!"

"Why are you talking this way? Just trying to help you, Martin."

"Help me! You had your chance to help me, but you left me lying out there, hurt. Left me to die!"

"What are you saying, Martin? I ain't done no such thing."

Martin was rising. Kane stared at the fresh blood on the man's hand, seeping between his fingers from some unseen, tightly gripped wound. "Leave me be, Spence. Just leave me be."

Martin finally made it upright and looked hatefully at Kane again. "You'll leave your partner to die," he spit out at Spence, "but you'll take in a hurt redskin. You're a sorry man, Spence. A sorry man, and no more a friend of mine."

He staggered to the other bunk and all but fell into it. Kane heard the creak of the strained bunk frame. Martin spoke again and Spence answered sharply, but this time Kane couldn't make out what was said. He couldn't focus his eyes. Queasiness struck again. He heaved and almost brought up the food he'd just eaten.

Closing his eyes, Kane let a feverish sleep overtake him. As he drifted off, he wondered again just where he was and what kind of men these were.

No answers to those questions were to be found over the next two days . . . or was it three days, or four? These were long hours of pain in mind and body, of perpetual sickness, of confusion and fever and images that came to Kane both when he opened his eyes and when his eyes were closed. Which images were real he could not say.

His recollection of those days would come back to him later only in fast, flashing memories, like scenes revealed suddenly by bolts of lightning, there and gone.

Flash.

Spence at Kane's side, face red with anger, voice muttering harsh words while he cleans up something reeking and foul. Kane, knowing he vomited, feeling ashamed that he did . . .

Flash.

The other man, Martin, sitting up in his bed, looking pale and terrible, thrashing now, yelling, accusing, arguing with Spence, who throws denials and curses back at him in a loud voice . . .

Flash.

Nighttime. The room lit only by firelight. Spence snoring on a floor pallet near the fire, Martin groaning softly in his own fevered sleep, Kane himself looking around, feeling better for the moment, stronger, enjoying a brief lucidity that brings him a quick comprehension that the place he is in is surely a line camp, a tiny outpost of some ranch, and that Spence and Martin are cowboys holding down winter duty here. The moment of clarity passing, fading into a nonsensical image of Kane's lost mother by the fire, stooping to stir something in a steaming kettle. Kane, overwhelmed to see her alive, calling her name, and her image vanishing even as she turns to respond . . .

Flash.

Daylight again. Martin and Spence shouting at one another like before, but this time with words Kane can understand. Martin accusing Spence of having seen him lying hurt in the snow but abandoning him. Spence strongly denying this, and telling Martin to lie still or else he'll reopen his wound, which is only just now closing itself . . .

Flash.

Spence at Kane's bedside, face close and lips moving, but his voice, seemingly coming from far away. "The fool did it himself, you know," Spence is saying. "Fell and stabbed himself with his own knife out there. Not my fault if he was lying hurt. Not my place to be his keeper, or his mama, or his nurse. The devil take him! I wish he'd died out there! He's been nothing but a misery to me as long as I've known him, and never more than now. I should have put a bullet in him while he was out in that snow! I should never have assumed the sorry old pestilence would die on his own. Should have known he'd come crawling back like a half-squashed roach, accusing me like I was some kind of murderer . . ."

Flash.

Spence's face again, even closer. "Tell me about the treasure, boy! You've been babbling about it again. Tell me, is it really the Punjab Star jewel itself? Tell me, boy! Tell me!"

Flash.

Night once more. Spence and Martin shouting at one another again in the dark cabin. Spence pacing about, waving his arms like a preacher, calling Martin a liar. The image fading, reappearing when the fire is a little lower. Kane staring, numbly watching as Spence leans over Martin, hands around Martin's neck, squeezing . . . Martin making no sound, his legs kicking, his hands vainly trying to push Spence away . . .

Flash.

Morning. Sunlight around the edges of the shutter. Sweat lying cold on Kane's forehead and drenching his pillow. Someone stirring on the other bed. It's Spence instead of Martin. Kane looking around for Martin, not seeing him . . .

Flash.

Spence at Kane's bedside again, looking down on him and nodding. Telling him that the fever is breaking and that he's going to live.

And calling him "partner."

Chapter 3

Kane sat propped up, eating slowly, taking small bites of one of Spence's biscuits. It was afternoon and snow was falling outside. Kane was weak, and his head hurt, though not as badly as before. His body stank, as did the bunk's foul linens. He'd sweated profusely, his body fighting the fever and delirium. His hair was matted and his clothing stiff with dried perspiration.

Kane swallowed a bite and took a small sip of water. He was still thirsty, though he'd been downing dipperful after dipperful of water since morning. His battle against fever and concussion had dried him to little more than a living human husk.

Spence was cordial now, pleasant toward Kane but still with that nervous intensity Kane had noticed from the beginning. Kane watched him as he moved about the small cabin, busying himself at small tasks that seemed to have no purpose beyond giving him something to do.

Kane took another bite, then laid the biscuit aside. His fever might be down, but it had ravaged him. The headache that had been with him ever since that train bandit struck him was like a steady, discordant humming in the back of his mind, so perpetual that he'd almost ceased to notice it.

With eyes closed, he spoke to Spence.

"You're a cowboy, I suppose."

"Figured that out, did you?"

"Yes. And this is a line camp."

"Smart fellow, you are."

"You're out here for the winter?"

"That's right."

"What do you do in a line camp all winter?"

"Mostly you just go loco from the lonesomeness."

"What work, I mean."

"Work? You ride the range, looking for cattle in trouble. Hurt ones, out-of-season calves. Cows bogged down in drifts or sinkholes. That kind of thing mostly. Or maybe you play nursemaid to hurt redskins, like I've been doing. I saved your life, you know."

Kane said, "I know. I thank you."

After a pause, Spence said, "There's a way you can show your appreciation."

Kane wondered what he meant, but did not feel the impulse to explore the question just now. Instead he asked, "Where's Martin?"

The pause was longer this time. "Martin?" Spence said, chuckling. "I don't believe I know what you're talking about, my friend."

Kane opened his eyes. Spence was standing by the fireplace, looking squarely at him.

"You must know," Kane said. "Martin . . . the

other man who was here. He was hurt, and you put him on the other bed over there."

Spence shook his head. "No. There's no Martin. There's been nobody here but me and you."

"But I saw him! I heard him!" A flash of memory came. "And I saw you argue with him, saw you . . ." The sentence went unfinished.

"There's been nobody but me and you," Spence repeated firmly. "You've been dreaming, son. Seeing things. Out of your head." He spoke slowly, enunciating each word. "Many things you may think you saw, you didn't see."

Kane frowned, staring at his feet.

"That kind of thing happens to folks who've been clouted in the head like you have," Spence said. "They see all kinds of images. But they're all false. Mirages. Not really there at all."

Kane thought deeply. "No," he said. "No, this was real. There was a man, he was injured. A wound in his side. His name was Martin, and you argued. He accused you of leaving him hurt out on the plains . . ." Kane trailed off, realizing both the imprudence and rudeness of what he'd just said, for he really knew no details, only what he'd heard . . . or was almost sure he had heard.

"Let me ask you something, boy," Spence replied. "After me taking you in, keeping you alive, feeding you, cleaning you up when I had to—do you think I'm the kind of man who leaves another to die out in the snow?"

Kane thought about it. "No."

"Then why do you give such credence to something you saw in the midst of a high fever, when it contradicts what you know of me?''

Kane thought, *That's a question worthy of a courtroom attorney.* ''I don't know. I suppose you're right. Maybe I just . . . imagined it.''

''That's right. You did imagine it. You've been feverish for days. Seeing things. You've laid there, raving. You've talked about seeing your mama. You've called the name of Toko, whoever or whatever a 'Toko' might be. You've called name after name—Porterfell, Blessed, Carolina somebody-or-other—and spoke as if they was all here beside you. Especially the girl. But nobody's been here at all but me and you. No matter what you think you've seen.'' He paused. ''Do you understand me?''

Kane looked away. ''I understand.''

''Good. Good. Let's be sure we keep it that way, eh? No more talk about this 'Martin,' all right?''

Kane paused. ''All right.''

''Good.''

Spence began busying around again, and for a couple of minutes there was no further conversation. Kane lay wondering if he really *had* imagined the person of Martin. It was possible. If he'd seen his own deceased mother by the fire, clear as the day itself, he might have seen other things that weren't really there too.

Spence spoke again, his voice now loud and cheerful. ''Yep, a man who's been hit in the head, and feverish besides, can see any number of things. Dream up all kinds of falseness that seems the truth.'' He cleared his throat. ''Of course, sometimes the very

24

opposite can happen, too. A man in such a state can have his tongue loosened. Speak freely of things he might otherwise keep to himself."

Kane wondered what this was leading to.

"Take you, for example," Spence said, turning to look at him. "You've laid there and talked about this Martin, who ain't real. But that treasure . . . I don't believe there was any nonsense in that."

"I don't know what all I might have said," Kane replied. "I'd not give much heed to it if I were you." It was hard to talk. His throat hadn't felt so scratchy since he'd nearly burned himself up in a hotel fire in Dodge City, Kansas, on an earlier leg of his lengthy adventure.

"Son, you've laid there and talked over and over again of this here treasure." He chuckled, his eyes growing bright. "You know what you said? You said, more than once, 'Punjab Star.' "

Kane picked up his biscuit and nibbled at it some more. Spence stepped closer.

"You know, don't you, son? You know where that stone can be found."

Kane wasn't about to admit anything to this man, even if he did owe him his life. He rather doubted that Spence was the kind to be trusted.

"What's the Punjab Star?" Kane asked, curious about how much Spence knew.

"Don't play games with me, son. We both know what the Punjab Star is. It's a diamond. Biggest diamond ever found. Named after the place it was dug up, nigh a century ago. Almost the size of a man's fist, and sparkling blue, like pure water in a moun-

tain lake. A legend and a lie, some say, but others
declare it's real. Just lost. Been lost for years. The
man who's lucky enough to find the Punjab Star one
day will be wealthy as a king, they say. A man could
live out all his days in splendor from what the Punjab Star would bring him . . . if he could find it."

Kane asked, "How do you know so much about
this?"

Spence grinned. "Funny you should ask that." He
crossed the little cabin to its far wall. The logs that
made up the wall were hewn flat on the inside,
chinked with mud and dried grass, and the whole
surface papered over with old newspapers to insulate
against the Montana wind. Spence tapped one newspaper that was pasted at a cockeyed angle.

"This is how I know," he said. "You ever been
stuck in a place like this for a long time alone, boy?
Let me tell you, you'll take to reading everything you
can find, again and again. You're surprised I can read
at all, ain't you! Well, I can. And one story here I've
read many a time. It's a story took from some Kentucky newspaper, it says. MYSTERIOUS LEGEND OF THE
PUNJAB STAR, the headline reads. FABLED BLUE DIAMOND
LONG-LOST, BELIEVED BY SOME TO BE STILL IN ENGLAND, BY
OTHERS TO HAVE BEEN STOLEN IN KENTUCKY DURING WAR.
I've read this story right off the wall, until I could
almost recite it for you. So you can figure why I
found it mighty interesting to be riding out in the
snow and find me a hurt redskin lying there in the
cold, hurt and sick and babbling out of his head
about the Punjab Star."

Kane felt quite uncomfortable about what he was

hearing. He'd been babbling about the Punjab Star when Spence ran across him? That seemed odd. Kane's quest, in his own mind, had little to do with the missing diamond. This was about finding the father he'd never known, not about locating the Punjab Star.

But if he'd been talking about the diamond in his delirium, maybe, somewhere inside, he was thinking more about the possibility of finding it than he had realized.

Spence came near to Kane, trying to look friendly but mostly looking intense . . . hungry. He dropped to one knee at the side of Kane's bunk and spoke earnestly. "I like you, boy. Never had much dealings with the redskin breed before, but I got nothing against your kind, and you in particular I find to be a good fellow."

Kane wondered how Spence could hold any view of him at all, considering he'd done nothing in Spence's presence except rave, babble, vomit, and sweat.

"Kane, I'll just talk straight and honest to you. I've heard enough from you since you've been here to know that you're on the track of something. Something big. The Punjab Star."

"I have no memory of ever saying anything to you."

"I don't doubt it. You were burning with fever, so hot you could have burst aflame. But you talked clear enough at the time. You sat up right in that bed, you talked to me face-to-face, and you told me all about what you're doing, how you're bound for Helena, looking for your father, how you've got some kind of coded letters put to memory, and how they'll lead you and your father to the Punjab Star. You said it all to me, clear as crystal."

Kane was dismayed. How could he have said so much? Yet Spence couldn't be bluffing. He couldn't know the facts he had just stated if Kane hadn't told him.

"Tell me straight, boy. Am I right? You and your pap are on the track of the Punjab Star?"

"I'm feeling sick again," Kane said. "I need to rest . . . don't want to talk right now."

"Answer my question, and I'll let you alone. Are you on the track of the Punjab Star?"

"I wish I was. I could make good use of a treasure like that."

Spence narrowed his eyes and examined Kane, evaluating him. "We'll talk more about this, you and me."

"There's nothing to talk about."

"I believe maybe there is. But I don't fault you for not wanting to talk about it. But in time, you'll own up." Spence stood. "You Indians drink coffee?"

"Yes."

"Got some Arbuckle on the shelf yonder. I'll boil some up. Maybe it'll help you shun that fever away. Sometimes you can fight the hot with the hot, you know."

"Thank you."

"Yeah, I'm going to be kind to you, Kane. Because I like you. And because you need help from somebody just now. Shelter and food and hot coffee, a good place to sleep. You need a partner, that's what you need. And a partner, my friend, is what you've got."

Spence went about his coffee-making in a rather showy manner. When the brew was boiling and the scent of it hung thick in the cabin, he poured Kane a cupful and brought it to him. Meanwhile, Kane's fever was definitely growing again. He could feel it rising inside him.

Spence said, "I'll help you sit up—there we go. Getting stronger, I think. You'll be fit to ride soon, yes sir. Just as soon as you shake off this fever for good."

Kane took the coffee. "I have no horse."

"Sure you do . . . as long as you're with me. I've got plenty of horses. Partners on a venture of common gain help each other out. Share what they have."

A partner. A "venture of common gain." Kane felt bad for reasons beyond his prolonged fever.

"I don't know that I've really been looking for a partner, Spence," Kane said.

Spence's fulsome grin went away, and the quality of his voice changed subtly. "Just remember who saved your life, Kane. Just remember that."

Without another word Spence returned to the coffeepot and refilled his cup.

He was silent after that for a good while, sitting in the corner on a stool, staring up at the wall, at the yellowed newspaper there. Reading again the story of the legendary Punjab Star.

Chapter 4

Kane's second round of fever wasn't as bad as the first, but he grew quite ill anyway, sick enough that his mind and perceptions were affected once again. This time, along with hallucinations and strange dreams, came a runaway-train ride through memories of the past eventful weeks during which he'd been on the run.

In a distorted, sometimes out-of-sequence fashion, he relived the adventure that had brought him this far.

He saw his despised but tenacious enemy, Robert Blessed, who had taken him from his Indian Nations home, murdered his mother, and imprisoned him in St. Louis. Kane relived twisted versions of the adventurous escape and flight he'd undergone, pursued each step of the way by Blessed and his agents. Running toward Wichita, where he believed he would find his father. Learning along the way of the connection of this chase to the lost legendary Punjab Star, and the relation of the diamond itself, in turn, to the Confederate band of raiders of which his own father, and Robert Blessed, had been a part during the war more than two decades before.

And he relived the worst part . . . the deaths. Ugly, needless deaths, ultimately traceable to the greed of his pursuers. The deaths of good people, such as Cypress and Lewis Washington, whose only sin had been their willingness to help a young fugitive in need of a friend.

He did not know now whether he was still being pursued. He had survived a trying adventure in a Colorado mining town, where he had almost found his father. He'd come briefly into the clutches of his enemies, too, including Robert Blessed, but had gotten away. He didn't know what had become of Blessed. Kane was eager to believe that Blessed was no longer out there, pursuing him as before, but he was afraid it wasn't true.

The image of Spence strangling Martin remained with Kane, coming frequently, and more vividly each time. He remembered the tiniest details—Spence's gritted teeth, the dark shadows around him and the flickering of his shadow against the wall as his hands choked the breath out of a man he now swore had never existed.

But Martin *had* existed . . . he must have. How could so vivid a memory be false? Yet Kane wasn't quite sure, despite himself, because even now he saw shapes in the shadows, heard whispering voices in his mind that he knew were all products of the fever.

Spence, Kane noticed, never left the cabin for more than a few minutes at a time. If he had duties to his employer's cattle, he was ignoring them.

Meanwhile, the snow outside continued sporadically. The sprawling Montana landscape was blanketed and beautiful, but whenever Kane looked out the window he was disturbed. With snow all around, he felt shut off, isolated from the world and the quest that had brought him to the Montana Territory to begin with.

Back in Colorado, his father had left him a simple map—an invitation of sorts, to follow him to Helena. Kane wondered if Bill Porterfell was still looking for him there, awaiting his arrival. If so, he prayed he wouldn't give up on him.

Kane was determined to regain his strength as quickly as possible. He had to reach his father. And somehow he had to shed Spence. He might owe the man his life, but he didn't see how that obliged him to make him his partner. As for that legendary diamond, the devil take it! It might be for the sake of the Punjab Star that Kane's enemies had followed and harassed him, but the jewel had little to do with what drove Kane himself.

Kane slept.

The fever was almost gone, so sleep came easy. Restful, healing sleep, not the miserable tossing and writhing that came with sickness. If he dreamed, he had no memory of it.

He opened his eyes and looked up into shadowy darkness, broken only by occasional flickering yellow light. The cabin was quiet; Spence was probably asleep, but for once he wasn't snoring.

Kane felt better than he had since he'd been injured. He was nearly sure his fever was gone for good this time. His headache had declined by half or more. He could even touch the sore place on his skull without wincing.

He lay there a long time, enjoying the silence and the darkness. Faint whispers on the roof told him that the snow still fell. Initially he found this pleasant, but soon he began to worry. What if the snow kept falling, deepening, until he couldn't get away from here? The idea of a full winter in a line camp with Spence brought him no happiness. And his father would surely give up waiting on him and vanish forever.

He had to get away from here, and away from Spence, as soon as possible.

A wet, sloshing noise near the fire reached his ear. Kane sat up slowly, peering over to investigate its source.

Spence was sitting there, leaned over slump-spined on a stool, staring back at him through tired-looking eyes. The firelight cast a yellow glow over him. He had a whiskey bottle in his hand—the source of the sloshing sound.

No wonder Kane had heard no snoring. Spence was wide awake and drinking.

"Hello, Kane," he said. "You're awake again now, I see. Hope I didn't disturb you."

"What time is it?"

"I don't know. What does it matter out here? Time don't mean nothing in a line camp."

"Where'd you get the whiskey?"

"Had it stashed away. Ain't supposed to have whiskey at the line camp, but hell with it. The boss man ain't around to see, and ain't likely to be. A man's got to have something to entertain him in a remote little hell like this one." He took another swallow.

"What ranch do you work for, anyway?"

"Triple M. Belongs to one Mr. Charlie Birdsong. Some kind of name, huh? Birdsong." Spence made a trilling little whistling noise and laughed.

"Where's his house and such?"

"Long way from here. That's why he has these line camps. So folks like me can waste their lives sitting alone through a long winter, going loco and reading the newspapers on the walls until they know every word by heart. Sorry life, living at a line camp. I'd as soon ride the soup line as live this way." He raised the bottle and took a swig. "Won't have to do it much longer, though, right, Kane? Once we find that diamond, me and you both will be rich men. Rich as kings for the rest of our days."

My, how Spence had planned it all out! His vision of the future was clear and straightforward, with Kane right in the heart of it all.

No, sir, Mr. Spence, Kane thought. *It's not going to be like you think. I'll not have you push yourself that far into my life!*

"What if I told you I can't find the Punjab Star after all?" Kane asked.

"I wouldn't believe you. You've talked too much about it for me to believe that."

"Fever talk."

"I reckon. But when a man hears the same fever talk over and over again, he begins to take some heed to it. Why you asking this? Are you telling me you really can't find the diamond?"

"I don't know if I can. Not without my father, I can't."

"Well, I guess you and me ought to get to Helena as soon as we can, then, and find him."

Kane was trapped and he knew it. He was in no position to counter Spence's plans.

"It's a long ride to Helena."

Spence finished off another swallow, wiped off his mouth, and held the bottle toward Kane, who shook his head. Spence belched and said, "We won't ride all the way there. Just down to Smithtown. We can catch the train at Smithtown."

"I never heard of Smithtown," Kane said.

"Nothing but a train station, couple of saloons, and so on. Tell me: How will we find your father in Helena? You arranged a place to meet him?"

"No," Kane replied.

"So what will we do? Advertise in the newspaper?"

Kane greatly disliked hearing these constant *we* references. Suddenly his quest wasn't his anymore. "I'll think of something."

"Yeah. Yeah, we'll find him, me and you. Ask around the saloons and such. A man can find out anything by asking around the saloons." He took another swig, his eyes riveted on Kane. "Your father's white, right?"

"Yes. My mother was Cherokee."

"Yeah. Hey, how much you reckon we can sell

that diamond for? I'd wager you it's worth more than me or you either one could imagine."

"Look, there's no assurance that diamond can be found, even if I found my Father, even if we could decode the letters."

"They're in code?"

"Yes. Something like the code stage magicians use to send messages to each other without people in the audience realizing what they're doing."

"You can break this code, can't you?"

"I don't know. Someone can, I'm sure."

"Who the hell would send out letters in code to tell where a lost diamond is?"

Kane paused several moments. "I don't know. I truly don't. And the way things have gone for me, there's hardly been time even to ask the question."

Spence took another drink. He smacked his lips and wiped off his mouth again. "Sure you don't want some whiskey?"

"I don't drink much."

Spence, bleary-eyed, studied Kane. "I thought all redskins liked whiskey. You know, Kane, I like you. You are fast becoming a good friend of mine. Yes, you are."

Wonderful, Kane thought. *Now he's going to turn maudlin and sentimental. I despise drunks who get that way. Better that than him turning mean, though.*

Spence drank again and turned his head slightly away from Kane, staring into a corner. His lip began to quiver as the alcohol took hold of his emotions. "I had another good friend . . . lost him recently. Makes me sad to think of him."

"Who was he?"

"He was . . . never mind. Just a man. He was a good partner, up to near the end of his life. Then he turned on me."

"What do you mean, turned on you?"

"Got stubborn. Disagreeable. Didn't want to follow through a plan we'd made together, a way we could both get money. A lot of it." Spence looked at Kane again. "I'll tell you something. Big secret." His voice was beginning to slur badly. "I ain't the most honest man in the world. I ain't no pureheart. I've committed a crime or two in my day."

"Crime?"

"Yeah. Nothing real bad. Just robbing. And Mart . . . I mean, this friend of mine, he'd done the same." Spence leaned forward and spoke in a conspiratorial fashion. "Don't tell nobody, but we had plans, him and me, to rob a bank at Miles City. But he backed off. Changed his mind. No reason he should have done that. Hell, we'd robbed one before and never had no trouble. Got three thousand dollars or more out of it. Lived high on the hog for a spell. That was back in Dakota, a few years ago."

"Maybe he was scared you'd be caught this time."

Spence was in the midst of another swallow but nodded vigorously as he pulled the bottle away from his lips. "Yes, indeed, that's it. He was afraid. Turned cowardly on me. I'd say, 'Look at us, living like wretched cowboys, spending harsh winters out in line camps, poor as church mice, nearly starved while old Birdsong makes money off us. We can be rich if we rob that bank at Miles City. We can take some of

Birdsong's own money—I know he has some in that bank.' And Martin . . . I mean, my friend . . . would say, 'No, Spence, it's too dangerous. They'll catch us and lock us up.' Coward. That's what he was. A coward.'' Spence shook his head, a man disgusted.

"So what happened to him?" It wasn't really a question Kane had to ask, but he was curious to see if he was about to receive a confession.

Spence was quickly losing all self-control, talking freely. "I'm afraid he passed away."

"I'm sorry. How?"

"He just . . . quit breathing." Spence's face reddened. "You know what that sorry old boar did? Went out and got hisself hurt, out there on the plains. Fell and stabbed hisself by accident. Then he accused me of leaving him there to die! And that just because we'd had a falling-out over this bank plan of mine. Can you imagine that?" Spence shook his head again and took a small sip from the bottle.

"Is that how he died? The stab wound?"

Spence flicked his brows up, then down. "Yeah. I reckon that must have been it."

That, and the helping hands of a strangler. "I'm sorry you parted with bad blood between you."

"Yes. Yes, it's sad, it is." Spence wiped a tear away. His eyelids were beginning to look heavy.

Kane said no more to him for now. Within ten minutes, Spence's head had dropped to one side and he began to snore, the bottle of whiskey at last rolling out of his hand, spilling the remainder of its contents across the floor.

Chapter 5

While Spence snored, Kane lay back, his mind active. Everything Spence had just said confirmed that the murder Kane had witnessed was no hallucination. Spence had strangled his own partner—this after having abandoned him, wounded, out on the plains, only to have him reappear. Spence was a dangerous man, one from whom Kane wished to escape as soon as he could.

I have to try, Kane thought. *Maybe I'm stronger than I think. I'll probably not find so good an opportunity again, unless he has another bottle stashed away somewhere.*

He *would* try. His fever was gone, and his head not so sore. If he could dredge up enough strength, and keep his dizziness sufficiently at bay, he might be able to make it. He'd take one of Spence's horses, and food from the pantry crate in the far corner. He could put miles behind him before Spence even knew he was gone.

Kane took a deep breath and rose slowly. His head hurt a little more than it had earlier, but he attributed this to the intensity of his feelings at the moment. He stood, testing his balance. So far, so good. Moving about the little log hut, he gathered up articles of his scattered clothing and dressed himself. He found a gunbelt and pistol hidden behind the pantry crate, marked with the initials "M.B." He didn't know what the "B" stood for, but he'd bet the "M" was for Martin. Taking what food he thought he'd need to make it a day or two without stopping to buy supplies, he packed it away in a burlap sack he'd found, then got his hat down from a peg on the wall where Spence had hung it.

Spence muttered and rolled over, but did not awaken.

Kane noticed two rifles leaned against the wall. Hesitating, he reached for one, then hesitated again, and withdrew his hand. He didn't really want to steal any more than was necessary from Spence. The man had saved his life, after all—though Kane doubted he would have done so had he not been murmuring about the Punjab Star when Spence found him. The pistol would be sufficient weaponry; he would leave Spence his rifles, even though one of them was probably not really Spence's property but that of the partner he'd murdered.

Kane opened the door and looked out into the dim light of a just-born dawn. He hadn't realized the night was so far gone. The air was so cold it stung his face, and the snow was piled nearly knee-high. It was not snowing at the moment, though, and the wind was still. There'd be no hope of getting away without leaving a very clear trail in the snow, but nothing could be done about that, so Kane decided not to let it worry him. Spence knew he was Helena-bound, anyway. If he chose to follow, he could do so with or without a trail.

Kane stepped out into the snow and eyed the gray, overcast sky. Was he sure which direction he needed to go? How far away was the railroad, the nearest community? Could he arrive there by dark? The day was well on.

He circled around to the small corral and horse shelter, really no more than a large lean-to. There were four horses in all. Kane didn't know which was Spence's and which had belonged to the late Martin. And where were the saddles? He'd anticipated finding them in the shelter, but he didn't see them.

He stopped, leaning against the corral fence. His head throbbed and he was incredibly weak. The cold sliced through him, chilling him to the very core. He felt a shudder—whether just from the cold or from a rebirth of his fever he didn't know.

Leaning harder against the fence, Kane felt a surge of depression so great that tears came to his eyes. He couldn't do this. He was still too weak, too tired, even after all the time he'd spent in bed. Even the prospect of merely looking for a saddle was over-whelming. His brain didn't seem to be working right; he couldn't recall how to determine which direction he should travel.

He bowed his head and allowed himself to weep freely. Every sob made his head ache worse, and he was deeply ashamed of crying, even though no one was near to see. He didn't let himself weep for long. When he was in control again, he prayed. *Great Cre-*

ator, let me regain my strength. Let me get away from this man . . . let me find my father.

He lifted his head, sighed deeply, and trudged weakly back to the front door of the line camp cabin.

When Spence came around to the world of the conscious again, Kane was asleep on his bunk, and all things in and about the cabin were as they had been before. Spence groaned, the sickness of a hangover taking hold of him, and literally crawled to the other bunk. Groaning again, he fell asleep awash in his miseries.

It was nearly a week later before Kane felt he was strong enough to attempt another escape, but opportunity was lacking. By this time Spence had become weary of "nursemaiding" and was eager to be on his way.

In Spence's mind, Kane detected, it was all quite simple. He and Kane would travel together to Helena, locate Bill Porterfell with ease, break the code of the letters Kane had memorized, and pick up the Punjab Star virtually at their leisure. That any obstacle to this simple procedure should present itself was to Spence unworthy of consideration. It *would* go well, and easily, and in the end the diamond would be found, then sold for an amount of wealth Spence seemed to believe would be roughly comparable to the value of the entire United States Treasury, and divided evenly: fifty percent for the Porterfells, fifty percent for Spence.

Such a split, after all, was the least that could be done for the man who had saved Kane's life, Spence noted more than once with a humble expression on his face.

Kane longed to break free of this man, but didn't know how he'd do it. Spence's whiskey was gone, so there would be no more drunken stupors. Without the influence of alcohol, Spence was a light sleeper. The few times Kane rose in the night, Spence was instantly awake, quizzing him about what was wrong and why he was up. There would be no sneaking away again.

The snow had stopped falling about the time of Kane's aborted escape attempt and had not resumed. But a deep freeze had settled over the landscape, and very little snow melted, except a token amount warmed by the direct rays of the sun.

Like it or not, it appeared that Kane was stuck here and would remain in the company of Spence for the foreseeable future.

It was a sunny Tuesday morning when Spence announced to Kane that the time for departure was at hand. The next day, he said, he and Kane would set out on horseback for Smithtown. Thus Kane should ready himself and rest as much as possible for the remainder of the day.

"You'll just walk away from your work?" Kane asked him.

"What work? You call sitting out the winter in a damned line camp work?"

"What about Birdsong's cattle? In this cold weather, there may be a lot of them in bad situations."

"Devil take the cattle. I've given up the cowboy

trade. From now on I'm a treasure hunter. And after that, a man of wealth and leisure."

Kane resigned himself to the inevitable. He would put up with Spence for now but shake him off as soon as contact with civilization was made again. Meanwhile, he would rest and prepare himself as instructed.

He'd be glad to get away from here, even in the company of Spence.

Morning broke bright on the snow. All indications were that the day would be sunny. Kane, used to the relative darkness of the cabin interior, could hardly bear to keep his eyes open in the blinding white expanse of sun-drenched snow. He squinted, peering out painfully between his nearly closed eyes, fearing his eyelids would freeze that way in the biting cold.

Spence seemed unaffected by the brilliant light. "On the trail, Injun friend, on the trail! Off to become rich men, me and you. Partners! Spence and Kane. Sounds good, eh, my friend?"

Kane put a hand to his brow, like a salute, and squinted harder. His head felt like it was gripped in a vise. "Sounds good," he said, having no option but to agree for now. The sun seemed to be growing brighter by the moment. He lowered his head and looked toward the shadow cast by the line camp cabin, trying to find rest in spite of his bleary eyes.

"I got the horses saddled already," Spence said. "Ready for us to go."

"Where'd you keep the saddles?" Kane asked.

"Behind the horse shelter, under a big oilcloth. Why you ask that?"

"No reason." Kane paused. "Why do you have two saddles?"

Spence gave an odd little twitch. "You ask too many questions, redskin."

"If we're going to be partners, let me ask a favor of you, partner to partner: Don't call me redskin. I don't like to be called that."

A visible anger swept Spence like a sudden wind. "Why, you damned sharp-tongued . . ." He broke off when he noticed that a change had suddenly come over Kane. "What are you looking that way for, boy? What are you staring at?" Spence stepped closer, lifting his feet high in the snow. "You getting sick again? You look peculiar all at once."

Kane did indeed look peculiar. He was staring at something poking out of a nearby snowdrift. A broken, gnarled cottonwood branch, he'd initially thought. But it wasn't. It was a man's hand. Fingers bent, clawlike, frozen hard, the flesh beginning to darken.

"Martin," Kane whispered.

Spence's eyes followed Kane's. He looked at the hand, gave a little snarl of anger, and cursed softly. His eyes flicked back and forth between Kane and the hand, then he swallowed and shook his head.

"Cussed shame. Poor fellow, whoever he is, must have froze to death out here."

"No," Kane said. "No. You murdered him, Spence. I saw you. And you know who he is. That's Martin, the man you tried to convince me I'd never seen."

"What are you saying, partner? What kind of talk is that?"

A part of Kane knew he was being most imprudent to speak as he was, but the sight of the dead man's hand, and the confirmation it gave that what he'd seen in the night he'd really seen, filled him with fury that overwhelmed caution. "Don't call me partner. Don't do it. That dead man in the snow was your partner. If that's what becomes of your partners, I don't want to be one. I may have been sick, but I wasn't deaf, and I heard enough to know what happened. You abandoned that man after he'd been hurt, left him out on the plains, but he made it back to the cabin . . . and you murdered him in the night. I know you did it. You strangled him. I saw you do it. It wasn't fever. It wasn't something I just dreamed up. It was real."

Spence, angry again, swore loudly and drew his pistol. He aimed it at Kane's head and pulled back the hammer. "I ought to kill you."

At this moment, Kane believed he was seeing the true face of Spence, not the fulsome, friendly one he'd presented to gain Kane's favor. Kane looked him in the eye and said, "You'd best reconsider that. You kill me, and you'll never have that diamond in your hands."

Spence thought that over, cursed again, and lowered the pistol. "I didn't kill nobody. I don't care what you thought you saw."

Kane was looking past Spence now, squinting harder, his gaze fixed on the distance, at something that had just caught his eye from far away. "I see something now, Spence," he said. "Riders coming our way. Barely in view, but I can see them."

"Riders? What the . . ." Spence wheeled, looked, then let out a long and very vile string of curses. "We got to get away from here, Kane. Fast as we can."

For once, Kane was in full accord with Spence. From the moment he had seen those still-distant riders—three of them—heading in this direction, one fearsome thought had gripped him: *Robert Blessed.* He'd found Kane's trail somehow. And he was coming. With some new gaggle of hired confederates to help him.

"I'm getting the horses," Spence said, "and we got to ride fast. Got to outride them, whoever they are, for there'll be no way we can hide our tracks from them in this becussed snow."

"Can you tell who they are?" Kane asked.

"No. And I don't aim to let them get close enough for me to be able to, neither. Not with our friend in the snow there. I'll not hang for murder. No sir. What if them riders are the law?"

"I thought you said our 'friend' froze to death. Why would you be afraid of the law?"

Spence did not answer. He was already running through the snow toward the corral, where the horses waited.

Kane peered from beneath his shadowing hands at the oncoming riders. They were still far away, and moving slowly because of the snow . . . but moving. The sight of them filled Kane with a strange dread.

No one would venture this far, under these conditions, without the strongest of motivations.

Kane wasn't at all inclined to discover what that motivation might be.

"Hurry, Spence," he said. "Hurry."

He was beginning to wonder if he would ever be able to live his life again without somebody being in pursuit of him.

Chapter 6

Kane and Spence fled across the plains as fast as they could, but the going was slow because of the deep snow. Their horses moved with great effort, their breath steaming in double gusts from their flaring nostrils.

Kane's head throbbed with each step of his horse, and all the jolting about on horseback did nothing to help his lingering dizziness. He continued to squint against the brilliant light, too, which seemed to intensify the sun's usual illumination fivefold. Though he'd forgone wearing his hat because of his skull injury—Spence had added a leather thong, looping from side brim to side brim, so that Kane could let the hat hang behind him, between his shoulder blades—Kane decided now to wear the hat despite his concussion, just for some relief from the sunlight.

As they rode, Spence continually kept looking behind him, toward the slowly receding line camp cabin, and cursing the snow because of the big, furrowed trail it caused them to leave behind. If whoever was coming out to the line camp wanted to follow them, it would be quite easy.

"Where are they now?" Kane asked Spence, who'd twisted about in his saddle again, eyeing the distant riders.

"Too cussed close!" Spence replied. "Three minutes, they'll be at the line camp. Four, they'll be on our trail, and we ain't even topped that first rise yet!"

"Can you tell if they've seen us?"

"I don't think they have. They're continuing on toward the camp, and if they'd seen us, I think they'd be veering our way."

With no more words for the next couple of minutes, Kane and Spence rode on, urging all the effort they could out of their horses. At length they reached the crest of a gentle, long swell of land that, once crossed, would at last put a physical, visual barrier between them and the line camp. But Kane had to wonder what use that would really be, considering how easily they could be tracked. Still, he made for the far side of the swell as if it were shelter from a fierce storm.

He was cheered to see that the wind had blown the drifts significantly on this side of the swell, creating a wide gully where the snow wasn't nearly as deep. Along this route they could increase their speed greatly and perhaps gain a vital lead on whoever was after them.

And who could it be but Blessed? Kane had been pursued so hard, so relentlessly by his jewel-hungry enemy, all the way from Missouri, through Kansas, then Colorado, that he had no trouble at all believing Blessed had tracked him here to this remote line camp. It appeared to him sometimes that Robert Blessed would track him, if necessary, right to the very door of hell itself.

To his surprise, Spence pulled his horse to a stop. Kane did the same, confused.

"Let's ride, Spence!" he urged.

"I'm a fool, Kane," Spence replied, digging in one of his saddlebags. "I plumb forgot about . . . this."

From the saddlebag he pulled some sort of stumpy pipe. Kane eyed it, puzzled, then recognized it for what it was when Spence took hold of one end and telescoped it out.

Spence heeled his horse back up the rise to a point that allowed him to see the riders, who were now at the line camp, dismounting. He put the spyglass to his eye—Kane noted with a certain chill that the name "Martin" was scratched onto the side—and peered across the distance.

"What are they doing?" Kane asked.

Without answering, Spence took the spyglass from his eye, slapped it closed, and moved his horse to the crest of the rise. Waving his hand above his head, he yelled, "Dominick! Here, you old coon dog! Come over and see old Spence!"

"Who's Dominick?" Kane asked.

"A fine old friend," Spence replied. "Boy, we been running from nothing."

"What about the others with him?" Kane asked. "Do you know them?"

"Nope."

"Is one of them a big man, graying beard, maybe a slight limp if he's afoot?"

"No, nobody like that," Spence said. "Whoever they are, if they're with old Dominick, they're all right."

Kane wasn't so sure. He'd been pursued by too many, for too many miles, to trust any stranger. But like so many other things just now, this was beyond his control.

Kane slumped in the saddle, enjoying the touch of the sun despite the cold, and squinting in the brilliant white light, awaiting whatever would happen to him next.

As the three riders, who had heard Spence's call, came over the rise, Kane was immensely relieved to see that none of them was Robert Blessed. And though he received some puzzled looks from the newcomers, nothing in their manner suggested that they had come here in search of someone matching his description. Thus he felt confident that these men, whoever and whatever they were, were at least not agents of Robert Blessed.

There was obviously a strong bond between Spence and the one named Dominick, a lean, tall fellow with deeply tanned skin and thick gray hair that spilled out from beneath the flat brim of a round-topped felt hat. He and Spence made their reacquaintance with much banter, backslapping, and broad grinning, while the other two men who had come with Dominick stayed in their saddles, quiet and observant, with similar looks and manners that told Kane they were probably brothers.

"Dominick Jones, you nigh scared me to death, coming out here like this!" Spence said. "When I seen riders coming out across this way, I had the strongest feeling that there was nothing good to come of it. Reckon I was wrong."

"Reckon you were. Hey, we found your partner lying up there in the snow, dead and stiff as stone. What was his name . . . Martin?"

Spence cast a quick, guilty glance at Kane. "Yeah, Martin. Had an accident, I'm afraid. I laid him out in the cold to keep until he could be buried. But never mind him. What brings you here?"

Dominick glanced at Kane. "Before I talk free, I need to know who I'm talking in front of."

"This here is Kane. Kane Porterfell. Half-breed friend of mine. My new partner."

"Line camp partner?"

"No, no. Kane don't work for the Triple M. Don't work for nobody but himself. And now me and him are working together."

"I see." The way Dominick was eyeing Kane made Kane wonder if Dominick thought him a deaf mute for some reason. He looked at and talked about Kane as if Kane were oblivious to it all. "But not cattleman's work, eh?"

"Not hardly."

"What I come to propose ain't cattleman's work, either."

"How'd you know where to find me?"

"Asked at the ranch. The cook."

"Oh, yeah. Well, you caught me just in time. If

you'd come a day later, you'd have found me and Kane long gone from here."

"Giving up your line camping job without notice?"

"You could say that. Pshaw! They ought to be glad to be rid of me. The truth is, I ain't took well to this job. Riding miles in the cold, rescuing cows and skinning them that can't be rescued and such as that ain't my notion of how to spend a long, cold winter."

"Speaking of cold, Spence, I'm ready to get out of it. Reckon we could go back to your cabin there and build up the fire, maybe eat a bit? We're about half froze, and empty as can be."

"Reckon we can go back. Why not? Kane and me have places to go, but I reckon a man can visit with old friends for a spell."

Kane was not happy to hear this. He wanted to go on, and he didn't have a good feeling about the character of these newcomers.

Dominick eyed Kane. "You sure he's all right? I've always been of the view that a redskin is bad luck. Same with your Chinamen."

"Kane's not bad luck," Spence said, laughing. "No sir. This is the biggest good-luck redskin you'll ever see." He winked at Kane, who felt a burst of insult and disgust to hear himself and his heritage discussed this way. He strongly wished that he could snap his fingers and transport himself far away from here, from these men.

Why had it had to be Spence who'd saved his life? Why not somebody else—*anybody* else?

"Who are your partners there?" Spence asked, eyeing the still-mounted companions of Dominick.

"Spence, meet the Rance brothers, Bub and Mickey. Good friends and partners of mine in a little venture we've got in mind. We'll talk it over more when we get back to the cabin and put some warmth in our bones."

"Let's go. But what's your 'little venture'?" Spence asked.

"We want to rob us a train."

Spence built up a new fire on the hearth and heated up the little woodstove as well, filling the line camp hut with a delicious warmth that Kane couldn't help but enjoy, despite the fact he despised being back here. He'd been ready to move on, to get back to his interrupted quest—and to figure out how to shake off Spence in the process.

Now, here he was, back in the same old line camp, with three new intruders into his life who were just as uninvited and questionable as Spence himself. It was discouraging. But at least for the moment he was warm. Still, he imagined his father waiting around for him in Helena, growing restless and deciding Kane would never come, and then giving up and moving on.

"Rob a train, you say?" Spence was saying. "You may not know it, Dominick, but it's already been done. A train robbery on the Northern Pacific line some days ago is what brought Kane there to me. He had a row with the robbers and they knocked him in the head and hauled him miles out onto the plains to die in the snow. He'd have done it, too, if I hadn't have saved him." He said the last line proudly, and Kane felt irked.

"I do know it's been done—it's that what gave me the notion," Dominick said. "I'd heard about that Northern Pacific robbery . . . and it come to me: They'll never be looking for another one to strike anytime soon. So now's the time for an enterprising man to gather himself some good partners and do the job. And it made me think of you, Spence. For I knew you had no ambition to be living the life of a cowboy forevermore."

"Amen to that, brother."

"The Rances here, they've got a bit of experience. Robbed a couple of trains over in Missouri, and a bank or two as well . . . you sure this redskin is safe, Spence? I find myself hesitant to speak before him."

Kane couldn't keep quiet. "I don't like being called a redskin. My name is Kane. And though it makes no difference to me, maybe it will to you to know that my father is a white man."

"So you're not a full-blood redskin. Just a half-breed. All the same to me," Dominick said. "Injun blood is Injun blood, no matter what the mix."

"I'd advise you not to insult my partner," Spence said with surprising firmness. "Me and Kane are in a venture together . . . one that, I have to tell you, could mean a lot more money than this train robbery you have planned could ever bring in."

"What kind of venture?"

It was Spence's turn now to be hesitant to speak.

"Don't know as I want to say, considering that some of the company here is new to me."

"You can trust me and my brother," said Bub Rance, whose eyes had turned quite keen upon hearing that Spence was onto a scheme with more potential return than a train robbery.

"No offense, but I can't know that."

"So what are you saying, Spence? You have no interest in joining up with us?"

"I'm saying I've already got fish of my own frying, and there's only so much room in the pan."

"Hell, Spence, we've gone to a lot of effort to find you. We've rode mile upon mile to get here, and had to track you down just to do it. It ain't easy to find these line camp cabins, you know. We spent two days looking the wrong direction, and Mickey there almost got the chilblains in his feet."

"It ain't that I don't appreciate you wanting me in with you," Spence said. "I appreciate it a lot. It's that a man has to set his priorials."

"His what?"

"His priorials. What thing's more important than the other thing, you know."

Priorities, you fool! Kane thought, surprisingly annoyed by Spence's misspeaking. *Priorities! If you're so determined to sound intelligent and important, at least learn the right words.*

"So just what is this big job you and your pet half-breed here have going?"

Spence rubbed his chin. "Well . . . I don't know if I should speak too much . . ."

"Spence, if you've got something that big, maybe

we ought to go in on it with you and forget about this train robbery idea."

"Well . . . what we've got is big, that's for sure," Spence said, and Kane was dismayed to detect just how much Spence was enjoying being the one with the big plan, the man who knows the secrets. A man in such a position was vulnerable to giving away too much, just for the sake of inspiring the awe of others. And Kane didn't want these lowlifes attaching themselves to him.

"Well, Dominick, though I'd truly love the opportunity to work with you again, I just don't know that it's something I'm free to do. It's Kane here who knows where the treasure is to be found."

"What did you say? Treasure?" Bub Rance piped up, his eyes, along with those of his brother and Dominick, turning at once upon Kane.

"What kind of treasure are you talking about?" Dominick asked.

"A big one, that much I'll say," Spence replied, deep in the pleasure of possessing important and coveted information.

Shut up, you fool! Kane was thinking. *Every word you say here could threaten my safety, and my chance to find my father!*

"A big treasure . . . and this half-breed can lead us to it?"

"He can, but not alone. We have to find his father first."

"His father? Who's that?"

Kane could have wept, watching Spence spill out dangerous fact after dangerous fact to men who gave no impression of possessing any excess of scruples. Was it not enough that he had to worry about being chased down by Robert Blessed? Must he now deal with this collection of prairie trash as well?

"His name is Bill Porterfell," Spence said, as Kane had known he would. "He's in Helena, and Kane and I are going to find him, and together with him, put our hands on the Pun—on the treasure."

"What were you about to say?" Dominick asked. "What is this treasure?"

"Maybe I'll tell you . . . later," Spence said. He drew in a deep breath and arched his brows haughtily.

Kane closed his eyes, shook his head, and asked the Good Creator above why fate had to deal him such a blow just now.

All he sought, all he wanted, was to find the father he'd never known. Why had any of this had to happen? Why had that train robbery had to intrude itself? Why couldn't he have gone on into Helena, as planned, without incident, and there found his father?

He knew that no answers to these questions would come. He also knew that there would be no leaving this place today.

Instead, the day would be worn away with Dominick and the Rance brothers pumping Spence for information, and Spence enjoying the entire process.

And bit by bit, he would give away all the facts he'd unfortunately come to know, and the end result for Kane would be more manipulation, more danger, and far less chance of ever seeing his quest come to a happy end.

It was disgusting. He rose from his seat and cast himself down on his bunk, where he lay staring at the wall. He could feel the eyes of the three newcomers almost constantly upon him. Piercing, hungry, and full of a lust for treasure that Spence was stirring within them with his cagey and unthinking words.

Chapter 7

Kane was actually slightly surprised to make it through to the next morning without incident or harm. He'd spent a long night listening to the snoring of the four other men crammed into the undersized cabin, expecting at any moment that someone would jam a knife or pistol against his neck or head and tell him to reveal the information he possessed or die on the spot. But it never happened.

As Kane had feared, Spence had spilled all the information, a little at a time. By midafternoon, Dominick and the Rance brothers knew that the knowledge Kane possessed was in the form of memorized letters and that these letters were in a code that, at the moment, Kane himself didn't know how to break. They also knew that the information he possessed was incomplete and that only by combining the contents of the memorized letters with what Bill Porterfell knew could the location of the lost treasure be learned.

By suppertime the others knew that the treasure was the famed and fabulous blue diamond, the Punjab Star.

In the brief time he allowed himself to sleep that

night, Kane dreamed that he was running down the middle of a street in a very ugly, empty town, pursued by a vast crowd of hungry-looking men, all of them with eyes that gleamed with the blue light of the Punjab Star itself.

And ahead, always just out of plain view, was the lone figure of his father, always receding even as Kane himself advanced and the grim army behind him gained ground.

They set out for Smithtown the next morning, retracing the path that Kane and Spence had covered the day before. Five mounted men, horses trudging through deep drifts of snow. Kane was solemn and acquiescent, realizing that he was trapped and there was nothing he could do about it. Spence turned rather serious, beginning to realize that merely for the sake of having others dote on his words he'd betrayed important facts that he'd have been best off keeping to himself. The Rance brothers, their thoughts hidden behind blank expressions, stared at Kane with eyes like those of hungry dogs. And Dominick Jones, with his small, vague smile and eyes that darted back and forth from man to man, kept his thoughts entirely to himself.

The miles fell away behind them, the level of accumulated snow diminishing as they moved south. The horses, growing accustomed to traveling in these conditions and invigorated by the cold, performed excellently. Kane's eyes had at last adjusted to the brilliance of sunlight on snow. And his headache was almost gone, his dizziness noticeable only when he moved his head too quickly.

They passed within sight of a couple of other line camps, and eventually a few distant ranch houses. The landscape was spectacularly beautiful; Kane decided that the Montana Territory was surely one of the finest places a man could hope to see. Despite the company he was forced to keep, he was for the moment quite happy to be back on his quest.

Now, if only he could figure out how to shake off these hangers-on.

The community of Smithtown, reached at last, provided little worth looking at. It was a railroad-stop community, standing on flatlands that flanked the Northern Pacific track. A store, a few houses, a scattering of barns and corrals, a water tank, a couple of saloons . . . that was about it. But for Kane it was a welcome sight. Lost out there in that distant line camp, he had begun to feel as if he would never see any sign of civilization again.

They were dismounting at a livery, where the horses would be rested, fed, and groomed, when Spence sidled up to Kane, somewhat away from the others, and said, "There's something I want to ask you."

"What is it?"

"The other night, when I was drinking . . . what all did I say about my old partner?"

"Martin? The man you at first told me didn't exist?"

Looking unhappy, Spence nodded.

"You told me pretty much everything, Spence.

That you and he once robbed a bank together, that lately you'd had a falling out with him, and how he finally died on you."

"I said all that, did I?"

"You did."

"Well, I hope you know I was telling you the truth."

Kane knew nothing of the sort. He had too vivid a memory of Spence leaning over Martin's bed, choking the life out of him. Kane had witnessed a straight-out murder, the kind that could end in a hanging if the case ever made it to the courts. And Spence surely knew it.

Kane wondered if the thought already played in Spence's mind of perhaps later getting rid of this half-breed who knew too much.

But if he wants to be rid of me, he can't do it now, Kane thought. *Not if he wants me to lead him to the Punjab Star.* Once again, ironically, his knowledge of those encoded letters was simultaneously a peril and a protection for him.

There might be another positive aspect of this, too, he realized. If Robert Blessed showed up, he'd have a fine time getting his hands on Kane with this gang of ruffians already claiming possession. Kane found that thought rather amusing.

When the horses were dealt with, Kane turned to Spence. "What now?"

"Got to find out when the next Helena train comes through," Spence said. "We'll have to ship the horses with us. You got no money at all on you, I reckon."

The cash hidden in the lining of Kane's coat suddenly began to feel heavy. "No. I'm sorry. What little I had was taken from me during the robbery."

"Yeah. Well, we can scrape it up between the rest of us. You'll be providing more than your share once you lead us to that diamond, right?" Spence grinned. "Going to be a pleasure, being rich."

Kane smiled and nodded, hoping his opportunity for escape would come sooner rather than later.

Spence made inquiries at the station house and came out looking mad.

"Cussed train won't run again until tomorrow," he said. "We'll have to spend the night here, waiting."

This brought a round of cussing, but it didn't take long for one of the Rance brothers to point out a brighter side: The saloons boasted signs saying they operated all night long.

"We can spend the night the right kind of way," he said. "Have us some drinks, some cards . . . there'll be plenty of chance for sleeping tomorrow on the train."

This proposal was heralded all round as a brilliant idea. Only Kane was sorry to hear it. Now that they'd arrived, he didn't feel as good as he had along the way, during the excitement of travel. His store of energy was rapidly being depleted, and he longed for a good bed beneath him and a pillow under his head.

"I don't know that I can abide being up all night," he said. "You know how weak I've been, Spence."

"Aw, you'll do fine," Spence said. "If you have to you can lie down on the saloon floor. I've done it before, more than once."

Kane didn't argue. He'd already decided that his

best survival strategy was to play along with these men and their big plans for the time being. That would give them more cause to trust him and would increase the chance that they would let their guard down later on.

The saloon was of surprisingly high quality for a train-station-community watering hole. Kane wondered how such a place could afford an authentic polished-oak bar with a heavy beveled mirror in a gilded frame behind it. The tables, though battered by much use, were also of good quality.

The five men found a table near the back and sat down. Dominick Jones lifted a hand and snapped his fingers. A few moments later, a barkeep with a well-waxed mustache came over, adjusting his armbands and grinning cordially.

"What for you, gentlemen?"

"A bit of your best liquid fire, my friend," Dominick said. "And make sure the glasses are clean."

"Clean as whistles. House guarantee," the man said. "Any food to go with that?"

"Crackers and cheese, if you've got it."

"We do. Back in a hop and skip, my friends." Whistling, he headed back to the bar. Kane found him likable, and wondered for a moment if this man might be of help to him, if he could somehow give him the word that he'd be pleased to be sprung from the company of his companions. No, probably not. What could one liquor-slinger do about his situation? Not much.

Kane ate the crackers but drank none of the whiskey. He knew the others would show no restraint, and they didn't, putting away shot after shot of the liquor. Before long, eyes were bloodshot and voices were louder, and the usually quiet Rance brothers were making Kane nervous by speculating about how many tries it would take to shoot the knobs off the big oak pillars that held the mirror in place behind the bar. He wondered just how wild this night might become if they kept on drinking.

An hour later, however, no pistols had come out, and all knobs remained in place on the mirror posts. Dominick Jones was showing signs of drowsiness, and Spence's head was bobbing on his chest, his numb fingers still curled around his shot glass.

Maybe, Kane thought, *they'll all get passed-out drunk, and I can slip out of here.*

But he didn't know where he would go, or if he'd have the strength required for such an escape.

He happened to be watching Bub Rance out of the corner of his eye when the man suddenly stiffened, looked at someone just then coming in the door, and cursed softly.

"What's wrong?" Kane asked him. Rance didn't acknowledge that he'd heard Kane; he just kept on staring.

Kane twisted his head and saw two men settling onto stools at the bar. One was a Texan-looking fellow with high boots, a broad hat, and white-gray hair that could have benefited from a cutting a month before. His mustache was equally big and untrimmed, adding greatly to the rough-hewn Texan look.

The other man, with an indefinable but odd quality about him, was broadly built and tall, with a clean-shaven but incredibly dirty face. Even dirtier were the buckskins in which he was clad from head to toe. Kane took in the sight for a moment, then turned back to Bub Rance, who was still staring at the new-comers, looking quite angry and dangerous.

Mickey Rance, who'd been deep in his thoughts and his whiskey cup, only just then noticed his brother's concern.

"What is it, Bub?" He followed Bub's stare across to the two men, who were getting the friendly treatment from the barkeep. "You know them two?"

Bub didn't answer, just stood up. He scooted his chair aside loudly and walked across the tavern toward the men at the bar.

"Uh-oh," Mickey Rance said, grinning. "Watch out. When Bub gets that way about him, somebody's about to find theirselves in trouble."

Kane had his back to the bar, but when he heard what Mickey said, he got up and moved to the other side of the table, taking the chair that Bub had just vacated. If there was going to be a fight, he wanted to keep an eye on the situation.

Meanwhile, Spence's head, which had been lolling to the left, rolled to the right as he snored and muttered. Dominick Jones, his eyes very red, seemed to be staring at nothing at all.

"What's going to happen?" Kane asked Mickey Rance, but Rance's only reply was to flash a hateful glance his way. Probably the kind who had no use for an Indian, Kane figured. He'd met many of that type in his day.

By now the pair at the bar had seen Bub coming and turned on their stools to await him. Bub strode up within six feet of them and stopped. He eyed the buckskinned one for a moment, letting his eyes come to rest on the pistol holstered backward on the fellow's left hip. Then he locked his gaze on the mustached one.

"Hello, old man. You remember me?" Bub's voice was loud. Whatever his business with this pair, he was willing to share it.

The old fellow squinted and looked Bub up and down. "Don't believe I do, son."

"Well, I sure remember you, you damned sorry old devil!"

"So I'm to be insulted, am I? I'd take offense, but because you're still a young man, and a stranger at that, I'm inclined to let it pass." The fellow turned around to the bar, showing his back to Bub, and to the barkeep said, "Buy my friend here a fresh glass of whiskey, or whatever he's drinking. Maybe that'll cool down whatever fire's got him so worked up."

"I don't want your whiskey," Bub said. "You turn around and talk to me!"

"You aim to shoot me in the back if I don't?"

"I'd do it! I'll shoot any varmint wherever he needs shooting—front, back, makes no nevermind to me!"

"Wouldn't advise you drawing on me," the old man said. "You might kill me, but Tru over here"— he tilted his head toward the buckskinned man— "would have you plugged so danged full of holes before you could even reholster your pistol that you'd not live long enough to have took any satisfaction in killing me."

"This is between me and you, O'Breen. You tell Buckskin there to stay out of it."

The old man turned to Bub again, brows quirking upward. "You called my name. Do we know each other, friend?"

"You ought to know me, O'Breen. You locked me up in your damned jail one night for something I didn't do. A hanging offense it would have been, too—and you had no grounds to accuse me. You decided I looked like the kind to take advantage of a ranch girl, and because of that you put me up and nigh got me killed by a lynch mob."

O'Breen's look was changing, recognition beginning to dawn.

The buckskinned man spoke. His voice was strange, quite whispery and hoarse, and only added to the odd but undefined and unsettling quality Kane had detected in him.

"You'd best get back to minding your own affairs and letting the past be the past, young man," the buckskinned man said.

Bub eyed the fellow. "I don't know you, mister. But if you don't turn around and leave me to my business, I'll get to know you right fast indeed."

"I wouldn't threaten old Tru," O'Breen said. "It ain't a wise man who threatens Tru. Howdy, Bub. I do know you. I can't say I ever expected to see you again. It's been a sight of years. You was hardly more than a boy then."

"Not been enough years. Not long enough for me to get over relishing the idea of seeing you bleed for locking me up when I was innocent."

"All I done was my job. The girl swore it was you who done that to her."

"She was a liar. And her lie, and you being willing to swallow it, nearly got me strung up."

Back at the table, Dominick Jones lifted his head. He looked about, left to right, squinting like a man trying to see through a fog, finally taking in what was happening at the bar.

"Hey, Mickey, what's going on with Bub over yonder?" he asked.

"I believe he's getting ready to kill himself somebody."

"Oh, hell, not now! That'll just cause trouble for us. Get the law all stirred up. I'm wanted here and there."

"I wouldn't try to stop him now," Mickey said. "He's gone over the line. And once Bub goes over the line, he don't get talked back across it again. Just sit back and relax. This may turn out to be worth watching."

Chapter 8

O'Breen stood and faced Bub Rance.

"Young man, whatever's past is past, and I advise you to leave it there. I do remember what happened . . . and I take no pleasure in the memory. Let's not revive it, all right?"

"I'm going to kill you, old man."

"There's no need for threats. Let's just turn around and forget about it all."

"Don't jabber at me like you're some old *compadre*. You almost got me killed, old man."

A bright redness slowly spread over O'Breen's face. Kane watched from the table and saw the old fellow slowly beginning to lose control. There obviously was an old and bitter history between O'Breen and Bub Rance, and Rance wasn't going to let it die.

The buckskinned man stood, clenching and unclenching his right hand threateningly, fingers drifting closer to the holstered pistol. Bub looked at him. "Don't even think of it," he said. "If I go down, I'll take the old man with me." And in a flash, Bub's own pistol was in his hand. Kane had never seen a true fast draw in his life; this one was almost as astonishing as a magic trick. He'd hardly seen Bub move his hand.

O'Breen went over the edge now, stepping fully between his buckskinned partner and Rance. The barkeep had lost his jovial manner the moment it became evident that there was going to be serious trouble between his two patrons and was now casting frequent glances toward a shotgun leaned against the wall behind the bar. Bub seemed to know what he was doing even though the barkeep was, at best, at the far corner of his field of vision.

"You, Smiley! Away from there!" he said, and the barkeep obeyed unhesitantly.

Bub was in a humor to toy with his victim. "Well, O'Breen, looks like I've got you where I want you," he said, smiling. "A lot different now, ain't it? You remember how you laughed at me when you threw me in that jail of yours? Remember how you said that jail was sound as a dollar, and nobody would ever break out of it . . . but how a hanging mob might find its way in? And me an innocent man!"

O'Breen spat back, "You weren't innocent . . . the girl identified you a dozen different ways. And you're wrong, Bub Rance: I'd never have let any mob in at you. I was a good marshal. I did my job and I did it right. There was no hanging mob. What I told you, I told you to put some scare in you. To keep you from trying to get away."

"Didn't work, did it? I busted out of that jail. The jail you said nobody could get out of."

"You did. I have to congratulate you for that. I didn't think it could be done. But what you done after you got out, I can't congratulate you for. You're a wicked man, and it's only too bad a hanging mob *didn't* get you. But what's past is past, and I'm ready to leave it behind. Why don't you just put that pistol down, walk away, and do the same?"

"Let me kill him," said Tru, in that strange, whispery, raspy voice.

Bub thumbed back the hammer of his pistol. Two others in the bar, nearer the door, bolted and exited.

Kane spoke up. "Isn't there some way to stop this?"

"I told you," said Mickey Rance. "He's crossed the line. Once he crosses the line, somebody bleeds. Can't stop it."

"Well, well!" Bub said. "You *congratulate* me for busting out of your jail! I never thought I'd have heard that from your lips, old man! Hey, I hear the council of your town gave you a bit of congratulations after I busted out. I hear they took away your little marshaling job because you couldn't keep your prisoners. Is that true?"

The old man's face was even redder now. "I'll abide your threats, Bub Rance, even your insults, but you leave *that* particular matter be. You hear me?"

"Then do something about it."

It all snapped right then. The old man reached for his pistol, but it was far too late. All Bub Rance had to do was squeeze the trigger, and he did, the pistol blasting at a deafening volume, the bullet tearing through the old man and barely missing Tru behind him.

Tru's draw, if it was really possible, looked even

faster than Bub's had been. The pistol was out and up and firing before Bub had time even to think of a second shot. It took the top of his head off and splattered the big mirror behind the bar with blood and brains.

Mickey Rance came to his feet with a roar and grabbed at his own pistol. Dominick, certainly past his somnolence now, reacted at once, pushing Mickey back against the wall. "No! No, Mickey! Ain't no point in you dying, too!"

Tru, having seen Mickey's reaction to his brother's death, was already taking aim and ready to fire. Mickey shoved Dominick away and pulled his pistol free. Cursing, he fired a shot at Tru, but Tru's pistol barked almost in tandem, putting a slug through Mickey's upper arm. His arm went limp at once, and the pistol fell from his hand.

Spence took a dive for the nearest window, smashed the glass and framing from it with his body, and rolled onto the street outside. Kane followed, not even thinking about what he was doing. He hit the ground hard, so overwhelmed with the impulse to get away that he didn't even feel the slightest twinge of pain in his recently injured head.

Back inside the saloon, gunfire played back and forth. Kane and Spence ran for the livery. Dominick came out the window after them, landing on his feet and falling in behind them. The gunfire continued, three or four shots more, then Mickey Rance made his own window exit and joined the flight to the livery, his recovered pistol now smoking in his other hand.

They found their horses and saddled them quickly. Only Mickey was unable to do so. He'd taken a second bullet in his lower left torso and was bleeding badly.

"Where is he?" Dominick asked, looking around the livery door, waiting for Tru to emerge. The sky was growing dusky, night fast approaching.

Spence and Kane were throwing on saddles as fast as they could. Kane would later marvel at how utterly unaware he was at that moment of his injuries and weakness. When a man had to, he could overcome a lot, and very fast.

Spence swung into his saddle, and Kane did the same. The liveryman, meanwhile, absent from the stable when they entered, now came in the back door. "Hey, now! You ain't paid yet for—"

Spence and Kane swept out of the livery, ducking low to avoid the top of the wide double door. They made a right turn and galloped out of town.

Meanwhile, Tru had emerged from the saloon. What accounted for the delay was impossible to say, but Kane later figured that Tru had been lingering over the body of his slain friend.

Dominick emerged from the livery, too, Mickey Rance behind him, riding double, bleeding and screaming in pain. Dominick turned and fired two quick shots at Tru, then spurred his horse and sped off into the night after Kane and Spence.

There was no snow except that already on the ground, but the air was biting cold, and the moon was high, illuminating the landscape so brightly that the riders could see a good mile or more. It was eerily beautiful, but Kane would remember little of the ride. Now that he had gotten away from town and his panic had subsided, he was feeling his head injury quite keenly.

As for the others, they were all quiet and somber, probably ashamed of having been routed by one determined, buckskinned gunman. Kane would later find some humor in the situation, but at the moment it wasn't funny at all. He'd felt the same terror as the others. Something about that raspy-voiced, dirty-faced gunman had been unaccountably terrifying.

Mickey Rance was suffering badly, leaning hard on Dominick, moaning and struggling to stay conscious.

"We're going to have to get out of this cold, Spence!" Dominick yelled. "Mickey needs to lie down and keep warm . . . and we may have to dig that bullet out of him."

"We're fools, all of us," Spence said. "We let one pistoleer run us off. We should have dropped him where he stood."

"We'd still have had to run," Dominick replied. "The law would have been down on us before morning." He paused. "Besides, that wasn't no regular pistoleer. That was the . . . *strangest* man I ever seen."

Mickey made a high, pain-racked sound that was like nails on slate. Kane winced; it made his head hurt more.

"Spence, we got to find shelter. You know this country better than any of us. Where can we go?"

Spence sighed loudly and looked around, benefiting from the bright moonlight. At length he pointed southwest. "About a mile that way there's a ranch owned by a man name of Breeding. An old Texan with an ailing wife. But he's known for keeping the soup line open and showing kindness to them that come by. We can maybe put up in one of his buildings."

"Let's go, then. I'm not sure Mickey's going to make it much further."

They rode on, less panicked now. If they'd been followed by the fearsome Tru, surely they'd have seen or heard some sign of it by now. Smithtown was miles behind them.

Kane shivered badly, feeling the cold slice through to his marrow. Having so recently been afflicted with fever and still not fully healed from his head injury, he had a harder time shaking off the effects of the low temperature than usual. He feared that much more of this would get him sick again, ranting and sweating, seeing images in the shadows, just like he had back at the line camp.

The mile that Spence had said they'd have to travel proved to be more like two, and those two seemed the longest miles Kane had ever traversed. At last, though, they saw the welcome sight of the Breeding ranch's buildings and fences out on the rolling plains.

"There she is," Spence said. "Looks mighty dark."

"I see no cattle or horses about," Kane said.

"I know," Spence replied. "I noted the same. Maybe the place is empty. Maybe Breeding's sick wife had to go off somewhere or something."

"Let's go see," Dominick said.

They rode on through the moonlight and drifted snow.

* * *

They could only suppose that Spence was right, and the cattleman Breeding had abandoned his ranch for the sake of his wife. Whatever the reason, he was gone.

So was any food the place had ever contained, and most of the furniture. From the looks of things, Kane and company were not the first set of travelers to take advantage of these free and open lodgings. There were signs of former inhabitants all around—empty cans, tobacco ashes and chewed-out quids on the floor, the shavings of some whittler, burned-out matches, and the like. Any sleeping done here, though, had been done on the floor, because there was no bed. The only chair in the place had a broken leg.

Their horses were in the corral, which was sufficiently neglected to have allowed grass to grow up in it, providing the animals something to crop at out there in the dark.

Mickey Rance was moaning and already fevered when they laid him out on a dirty blanket that Spence found wadded in the corner. Kane had no reason to feel any trace of pity for Rance, but he couldn't help but feel sorry for him because of the pain he felt, both from his wound and from losing his brother. Spence had started a fire in the fireplace, and lit a couple of old candle stubs he'd found on the floor. By the flickering light Kane looked down on the sweating, tossing, bloodied Mickey Rance and wished he could do something to ease the man's suffering.

Those tender thoughts diminished a little when Rance suddenly aimed a finger at Kane and said, "It's his fault! Damned redskins . . . they always bring bad luck with them!"

It seemed to Kane that Mickey Rance's bad luck had far more to do with his late brother's impetuous nature than with him, but he kept his mouth shut.

Kane wandered off alone to a far corner of the cabin, which was nothing but one huge room, and sat down, leaning back against the wall and closing his eyes.

He was tired, weak, hurting, and lonely. Right now he'd give any amount of money if he could spend just five minutes with Carolina Railey, being healed by her smile, her touch, her mere presence. But she was far away in Colorado, where he'd left her with her father. He would once again rejoin her when all this was over, and he was in the company, the Creator willing, of his own father at long last.

Would they have the Punjab Star as well? Kane didn't know and really didn't much care. Meeting the man who'd given him life would be enough for him.

He closed his eyes and tried to think peaceful thoughts—a near impossibility with Mickey Rance moaning and yelling, slowly going delirious over across the room. He was quite a different man now from that callous chortler who'd enjoyed watching his brother go "over the line" and spark a violent encounter.

Kane suddenly remembered a long-forgotten proverb of old Toko's: The man who laughs at the snake is the man the snake will try to bite.

Spence tended to Mickey, looking at the wound, talking kindly, trying to calm him down. Dominick paced about, restless, unhappy, obviously tormented by the sounds of Mickey's suffering. And he kept looking out the window, as if expecting to see the grim figure of Tru appearing like a vengeful ghost.

"I'm going to have to cut that lead out of you, Mickey," Spence said. "I'm afraid it ain't going to feel good, but it's got to be done. Have we got any whiskey, anybody? Any whiskey at all? I need it to clean my knife so I can dig that bullet out of him."

No one had any whiskey. What liquor they'd had still sat on the table in the tavern, except for what flowed through their veins, but that had substantially lost its effect. The fight in the tavern and the panicked flight from Smithtown had had a very sobering effect.

"Don't dig in me!" Mickey begged. "I can't bear the pain of it! I can't!"

"Got to get that bullet out, Mickey," Spence repeated. "Otherwise it'll kill you for sure."

"No . . . no, please . . ."

Suddenly Dominick said, "Listen!"

Mickey, unhearing and lost in his own world of misery, kept right on with his moaning and weeping. He was losing a lot of blood.

"Listen!" Dominick said again, louder. "There's somebody out there."

Kane straightened and opened his eyes.

"What did you say?" Spence asked.

"I swear . . . there's somebody out there," Dominick said. "You don't reckon . . ."

"I don't know . . . I don't know anybody else who would have followed us," Spence said.

Dominick looked quite rattled, but shoved his shoulders straight as a soldier's and said, "I'm going out there. I'm damned if I ain't right ashamed of myself for letting one gravel-voiced, buckskinned pistolero put such a cowardly scare in me."

"It may just be a straying beast you heard out there," Spence said, Mickey's moaning a steady undertone to the conversation. "I doubt anybody's followed us this far. Not as fast as we left that place."

"We'll see soon enough," Dominick said with forced bravado as he pulled out his Colt pistol, making sure all the chambers were loaded.

Kane, still seated, watched with tense fascination as Dominick Jones left the ranch house and vanished into the darkness outside.

Except for Mickey's suffering sounds, there was a very eerie silence about the place for a few moments. One of the horses nickered, sounding disturbed.

Just a dog, or a straying wolf, Kane told himself. Nobody would have followed this far in the dark.

Except maybe somebody who was sufficiently angry about seeing a friend and partner murdered before his eyes, a small and unwelcome voice inside responded.

"Where's Dominick?" Mickey asked, suddenly interested, for no apparent reason, in the world beyond his own pain. "Where'd he go?"

"He just stepped out a minute," Spence said.

"Did he go to get Bub? Where is Bub?"

"Mickey, don't you recall? We lost him. Bub got shot. Back in Smithtown."

"Shot?"

"That's right."

"Who shot him, Daddy? Daddy, get Momma . . . get her fast . . . somebody's shot Bub."

Spence looked over at Kane and made loco motions with his fingers. Mickey was worsening fast, already losing his good sense, entering delirium.

Kane nodded, then looked at the gloom beyond the unshuttered window nearest him. On the other side of the cracked glass panes, the night seemed oppressive and deadly. Kane noticed that the moon was coming and going now; clouds had rolled in, obscuring it one moment, revealing it the next. The landscape was alternately bathed in light and darkness.

He glanced over at Spence, who had his pistol out, his attention diverted from the pitiful Mickey for the moment. The door that Dominick had closed behind him held his full concentration.

Just then, Kane felt for the first time a sense of kinship with Spence. At this moment their interests and their dangers truly were unified.

Mickey's voice trailed away softer and softer, his moans becoming quieter, lower, with longer gaps between. His face was growing more and more pale.

The man was dying. Kane could both see it and feel it.

Outside, there was noise. No voices, no shots, no loud sounds of any kind . . . just motion, a faint thumping, sounds that Kane couldn't quite identify.

A soft groan at the end of it all, maybe, but he wasn't sure.

More silence ensued. Then, just as Kane was about to whisper a question to Spence, they heard bootheels on the porch outside. Someone was slowly crossing the boards.

The door creaked open.

Dominick walked back inside and closed the door behind him. He seemed very calm now, but even in the imperfect and shifting light from the fire and the two flickering candles, Kane could see the strange pallid look of his face and the dark wetness that stained the front of his shirt, all down his chest.

"I been stabbed, boys," Dominick said. He nodded down at his chest. "Stabbed right here, bunch of times. He just came out of the dark, like a ghost. The funny thing is, I don't even feel it. How can that be?"

Dominick closed his eyes and collapsed slowly to the floor. He let out a long, slow sigh, breathed deeply two times, and then breathed no more.

Mickey Vance let out a soft moan, almost too quiet to hear.

Spence looked at Kane. "Boy," he said, "I fear we're going to die here tonight."

Outside, in the darkness, someone was coming toward the house.

Chapter 9

Right then, Kane got mad. Righteously, purely mad.

Die here tonight? By no means. He hadn't come this far to see his quest—and his life—cut short in the company of a bunch of criminal fools.

By heaven, if he was to die here, he'd not do so passively. He would expend every effort he could to get away.

Kane rose, went to the prone Dominick, and took his pistol. Spence had his own pistol out, and looked uncertainly at Kane, whom he'd kept disarmed since the beginning.

"I'm going out there to get this Tru, whoever he is," Kane said. "I'm not going to sit and wait for him to shoot me through a window."

"I don't want to die . . . don't want to die . . ." This came from Mickey Rance, who was writhing and pale and clearly about to die whether he wanted to or not.

Kane headed toward the back of the house.

"Wait . . . he's out in front," Spence said. Kane had never heard anyone sound more scared.

"I know. I'll sneak around," he replied. He went

straight to a back window, hefted it up, and slid out into the cold night.

Poor Spence, he thought. It probably wouldn't go well for him at all once Tru got to him. But this was his fight, brought about by the acts of his chosen companions, not Kane's. And he would have to find his own way out of it. As for Mickey, it was already too late for him.

Kane did not circle back around the house as he'd told Spence he would. He had no intention of confronting Tru. Instead he loped out through the darkness, aiming on putting as much distance as possible behind him. The moon was still out, but a glance at the sky revealed that a massive cloud bank was now right at the moon's rim and about to move across it. The plains would be as black as ink; even in such a good tracking medium as snow, Tru would be unable to follow Kane as long as it was dark.

Kane could only pray that he'd not try to follow him come morning.

Kane still heard no shooting back at the ranch house. That meant Tru was probably still sneaking about outside, preoccupied with the pair in the house. Well and good. The more time Kane had, the farther he could run.

The bank of clouds hit the moon, dimming the landscape like someone had just cranked down the lights on a vast natural stage. So great was the difference that Kane was actually blinded for a couple of moments. He paused, letting his eyes adjust to the dark, and went on. The bank of clouds was huge; as best he could tell it extended to the horizon. Just what he needed.

He ran as hard as he could in the snow, so motivated that he hardly noticed the cold even though ice was forming around his nose and the corners of his mouth. His breath came hard, and his head throbbed, but not enough to stop him.

Gunfire sounded back at the ranch house.

Kane ran harder, fell, got up, and ran again.

He heard a horse's nicker nearby. No, no, not a rider, not somebody else in pursuit! He dropped to his belly in the snow, panting and peering through the inky night, trying to see whoever it was.

He heard the faint nicker again and made out the outlines of a horse, standing still. No one on it or nearby that he could see.

Kane rose, looking about. No sign of anyone.

Two more shots blasted back at the cabin. The sound was surprisingly distant. Kane realized he'd run farther than he'd thought.

He approached the horse, which was tethered to a scrub tree poking out of the snow. Whose horse was it?

Tru. It had to be his. He'd left it here and made a wide circle back to the ranch house.

Kane's mind raced. Should he take the horse? He played out the likely scenario if he did. Tru, if he survived the fight at the ranch house, would come back here for his horse and find it gone. Come morning he'd track it, probably riding one of the mounts Kane and company left behind at the ranch.

On the other hand, he might consider that gaining

several horses in this one's place was more than a fair trade and that a lone half-breed wasn't worth chasing.

And, if Kane didn't steal the horse, Tru might return here come morning and track him anyway. He'd be quickly overtaken, and by then his feet might be frostbitten.

He decided to take the horse, if for no other reason than to maximize the distance he could travel.

"Easy, easy now, my friend," Kane said soothingly, approaching the horse, which side-eyed him and snorted. "Be calm . . . I'll not hurt you."

Remembering how his mentor, Toko, used to calm skittish beasts, Kane sang gently to the horse in the Cherokee tongue, careful not to make any sudden movements.

More gunfire erupted at the ranch house. Apparently Spence was at least making a stand.

He didn't necessarily hope Spence would die. The man had saved his life, after all, and Kane owed him for that. If Spence did get killed, though, Kane reminded himself, it would be only justice for his murder of his partner back at the line camp cabin. Whatever happened—whether the man won this fight or lost it—this night would forever get Kane away from him.

And how could Spence possibly win? Tru was a fearsome foe, obviously tenacious and determined. He'd tracked them all this distance on his own and had knifed Dominick Jones with the silence of a phantom. He had blood to avenge, whereas Spence was merely panicked and struggling for survival.

Tru would win, no question of it.

Kane untethered the horse, gently rubbed the animal, then swung into the saddle. It was a good one, a comfortable fit.

As the unseen gunfight continued back at the dark ranch house, Kane rode out, heading in what he hoped was the general direction of Helena.

How long he rode he did not know. He simply sat on the horse, letting it plod on in virtually a straight line, letting the miles fall behind him.

Whether Tru would come after him he wasn't sure. It depended on how determined Tru was to punish every one of the party who had been involved in the fracas at Smithtown and on how much he valued this horse.

The entire sky had clouded over by now, making the night murkier than ever. But Kane's eyes were keen, and the snow provided some amplification of what meager moonlight there was. At length he topped a rise and pulled the weary horse to a stop, looking down upon another ranch.

This one was as empty as the one he'd fled, and in fact, the house was in ruins. Nothing but charred timbers, barely visible in the night.

But beyond it stood a stout, two-story barn, only partially touched by the fire that had destroyed the house. Kane sniffed the air and detected a lingering but faint scent of burnt wood. The fire, though sufficiently long past to smolder no longer, must have been relatively recent.

"Come on, friend," he said, urging the horse

toward the barn. "Or are you my friend? You might end up being the reason your owner comes after me. And I don't want to face him. He scares me."

The horse plodded down the rise. The burned-out ranch was a ghostly, eerie place. But Kane was edgy and exhausted and still worried about what the daylight would bring.

The barn had big double doors, but part of one had burned away. Kane dismounted and shoved them apart as far as the drifted snow would let him, creating an opening just wide enough to accommodate the horse. He led it inside, where it was as dark as a cave.

He'd hoped the barn interior would be warmer than it was. But the Montana cold had permeated it thoroughly, and the walls kept out nothing but the wind.

As Kane unsaddled the horse he noticed a feed sack tied to the saddle. From it he fed the hungry, tired beast. His own stomach was empty enough now that he might have eaten of the oats himself. But a search of the saddlebags produced some old biscuits and jerky that made for a much better feast. He made himself eat the food slowly despite the urge to wolf it down like a famished dog. And he made himself stop short of eating it all. Come morning, he'd be hungry again.

The wind was picking up outside, blowing through the damaged and partially open door, so when the horse had finished eating, Kane moved it into a stall where it would be sheltered.

He climbed to the loft, looking for a place where

he could nestle and hope to work up a little warmth. The idea of building a fire was appealing but also frightening. What if Tru had somehow managed to follow him despite the darkness? A flickering light seen through some gap in the barn wall would betray him.

Kane bunched his coat around him, pulled his hat low, and tried to rest. Meanwhile, he listened, for some telltale whisper of movement outside the barn, a whinny from the horse, anything that would reveal the approach of Tru. Kane tried to assure himself that it was unreasonable to believe Tru could have picked up his trail in the dark, but his fear lingered.

His mind drifted back, recalling another time he'd perched in a barn loft. Someone had come in; he'd looked over the edge of the loft and for the first time seen Carolina Railey, stopping in at the barn with her showman father for a rest and a meal.

She'd seen him up there but hadn't betrayed him. And she'd left some food behind for him, without her father knowing.

He smiled at the memory, hearing a faint cracking of ice on his lips when he did so. When he reached up and touched his face, he found it so cold that it had gone numb.

That's it, he thought. *I have to build a fire, no matter what the risk. Otherwise I'll freeze to death.*

Descending from the loft, he explored the barn a bit as best he could in the dark. He found another empty stall with a relatively clean earthen floor. In here, he figured, he could build a blaze that might not be visible from the outside.

Kane scrounged up straw, scrap pieces of wood, and anything flammable he could find. He had matches, but only a few, and when the first three of these failed to adequately ignite the straw he'd gathered for tinder, he sighed and did the only other thing he could think of.

From the lining of his coat he pulled a couple of bills, folded them, and after some initial and inevitable hesitation—this was *money*, after all—lit them with a fourth match. With these he managed to get the fire going and carefully piled up scrap materials until the blaze fully caught, filling the stall with a wonderful, healing warmth.

Kane sat back, letting the heat wash over him, and smiled again at the realization that he'd just used money to start a fire. Who could have imagined that a poor half-breed from the Indian Nations would ever have found himself doing such a thing? Money for tinder! Remarkable indeed!

But if I were to find the Punjab Star, Kane thought, *what I just did wouldn't even seem remarkable. I'd be so wealthy that no amount of money would seem like it amounted to anything.*

But I don't really care about that diamond, he reminded himself. *All I want is to find my father. And to somehow live a life that doesn't involve being chased and threatened at every turn.*

Another thought rose, however: *Once I do find my father, and if he really does have the final piece of the puzzle that could lead us to the diamond, would the Punjab Star matter to me then?*

He couldn't find the answer to that one. He'd just

have to wait until the time came to know. Life on the other side of finding Bill Porterfell was a dark and unmapped territory that could only be explored once he reached it.

Kane closed his eyes. He didn't fall deeply asleep, but he let himself relax and rest. His body was tired and aching, and his injured head hurt.

But he wasn't dizzy anymore, he noticed with pleasure, and there was no fever or sense of sickness. It appeared he actually *was* going to get past all of this.

At last Kane did fall fully asleep. The fire died down and the cold awakened him. He looked around, listening. Nothing was amiss. All was as before. He built up the fire again, got warm, and again fell asleep.

When he next opened his eyes, it was a little past dawn. He stared at the embers of the fire until he remembered where he was. Rising and stretching, he yawned, scrounged up some more wood scraps for the fire, and thought what a good thing it was to be alive and to have escaped that deadly battle back at the ranch house.

He wondered where Spence was. Dead, probably. About Mickey Rance's fate there was no question. He was already knocking on the dead-house door when Kane made his escape.

Time to move on, Kane thought. *If Tru intends to track me, he'll be doing it now. I need to put some miles behind me and, if possible, find some way to break my trail.*

Remembering the food in Tru's saddlebag, Kane

left the stall to go get it. Before he did so, however, he picked up the pistol he'd taken from Dominick. On these wild plains, a man could never be sure when he might encounter a wolf.

He stopped short in astonishment as soon as he was out of the stall door.

Standing in the midst of the barn, staring at him without words and with pistol up and out, was Tru.

Chapter 10

Kane stood like a statue for a moment, then pulled the pistol from his belt and leveled it at Tru. He'd not have done such a dangerous thing had he thought about it, but he'd been so surprised to find the buckskinned fellow there that thought had flown out the window, as it were, and instinct had taken its place.

Surprisingly, Tru did not instantly shoot him.

The pair stood there, staring at one another, pistols leveled, each one fully capable of killing the other but neither one doing it. Not yet, anyway.

"So you tracked me," Kane said.

"Yep," Tru said in that raspy, cold voice, rousing that inexplicable sense of disquiet that he engendered merely by his look and manner.

"How'd you do it in the dark?"

"Found my horse missing. Struck matches and found tracks, followed them a stretch that way, until I seen you was traveling in a straight course. I know this country and figured you was making for this ranch here. Burned down three weeks back. So I just come that way. Sure enough, here you are."

"I wasn't making for this ranch. I just found it by chance."

"Well, then, I guess I was just lucky."

"You going to kill me?"

"I ain't decided."

"I could kill you, you know."

"You'd just die doing it. However good a shot you are, I can assure you that before your bullet killed me, I'd find the strength to squeeze this trigger."

"Same here."

"Then maybe we don't need to be standing here holding these pistols on one another."

"Maybe not, but I'm not lowering mine."

For a few moments more they continued to stare at one another.

Kane asked, "Why didn't you just shoot me while I was sleeping, or when I stepped out of the stall?"

"Don't know I want to shoot you."

Kane stared at the odd person before him. "I admit I'm a little confused. But if you don't want to shoot me, that's good news."

The standoff went on silently for half a minute or so.

"Listen," Kane said. "Let me tell you who I am, and how I came to be with those men. All I am is a young man from the Cherokee Nation. My mother was murdered, just like those men murdered your partner back at Smithtown. Now I'm headed for Helena, because I believe I can find my father there. And if you're one of those who hates Indians, please know that my father is a white man. Maybe that'll make a difference to you."

Tru's eyes took on a strange, disturbing glare that Kane couldn't figure out. A look of hatred? Disbelief? Sadness? It was impossible to tell.

"You're looking for your father, you say?"

"Yes. I've never known him, in all my life. And I want to find him. But if you kill me, it'll all be over, and I'll die without ever having laid eyes on him."

That odd glare intensified. The pistol began to tremble in Tru's hand.

This is it, thought Kane. *I've said something that's made him mad, and now he'll kill me. Unless I kill him first.*

Kane steeled himself to shoot, and probably be shot, but something made him hesitate. What it was required a moment to register, and when it did, he was stunned.

A tear streamed down Tru's grimy face.

Tru lowered the pistol and put it in its back-turned holster. Then he reached up, swept off the big flop-brimmed hat, and lowered his head.

Thick, auburn hair spilled down, longer than Kane's own hair ever had been in the days before he hacked it short to try to disguise himself from his enemies.

Kane let his own pistol drop to his side and dangle there as he discovered at last what was the quality about this man that was so odd and disturbing.

It was that Tru wasn't a man at all. Tru was a woman.

* * *

In the little stall, with the fire built up higher, they talked. Now that Kane knew the truth about Trudy Marie O'Breen, sitting there with her hair spilling down all around, he couldn't fathom why he hadn't been able to figure it out before. But when she sighed, bunched her hair up, and put the hat back on, suddenly she looked quite masculine again.

No wonder he'd been troubled by her. He wondered if Trudy even realized that it was that disguised, muffled essence of her femininity, coming through her masculinized veneer, that gave her that disorienting, intimidating quality that stood her in good stead against antagonists.

"So Mr. O'Breen was your husband?"

She chuckled. "Oh, no. I've never had no husband. He was my brother."

"I see. I'm sorry." Kane tried to remember the details of the exchange between Bub Rance and O'Breen. "He was a lawman?"

"Used to be. Little town in Missouri. He told me all about it; these things happened before I knew him."

Before she knew him? Kane wanted to ask what that meant, but she was already going on with her narrative.

"He had problems there. He was a town marshal, paid right well, and kept trouble down like he was supposed to. But the jail was sorry, of no account at all. People busting out as quick as they could be locked up.

"Tom decided to fix up that jail, and he did it, paying for it all himself. Made it so stout he figured nobody could ever get out of it. And for a spell nobody did. Then one day he locked up this young fellow for having mistreated a young gal—it was your very partner back at the tavern, it appears—and Tom bragged that this fellow would never get out of that jail. And to scare him, he told him that he'd best not even try, for there was a hanging mob ready to string him up if he did get out.

"Well, this young man did try to get out, and danged if he didn't succeed. And as he ran, he stole a horse from a barn at the edge of town. Happened to find a young lady in the barn, milking a cow, and did some things a man ought not to do. That barn happened to belong to the mayor of the town, and the young woman happened to be his daughter."

"I see," Kane said. "And the mayor, no doubt, blamed your brother for it happening."

"That's right. I guess if Tom hadn't bragged that nobody could get out of his jail, it might not have been so bad for him. But he did brag, and so the mayor held him to blame for what happened. Made it hard for Tom thereafter."

She paused to use a twig out of the fire to light a pipe she'd just filled. Puffing strong-smelling smoke, she tossed the twig back in the blaze, set the pipe in her yellowed teeth, and finished out her talk with the pipe clamped there, the bowl of it bobbing up and down with the motion of her talking.

"After that, a couple of other prisoners managed to break out of the jail, too, and Tom just got to be plain old despised by the mayor and the town council. He took to drinking, trying to fight his worries, for he needed the job and feared he'd lose it, and that just made it worse. When they caught him drunk at his office one day, they sent him packing. Tom took to drinking all the more, roaming around, finding work here and there, in this marshal's office or that sheriff's office, but never making much of himself. Then I found him, and we took up together, and he pretty much quit drinking at all, with me helping him along that way, you see. Here lately, Tom hardly touched a drop, and he'd never let himself get drunk." She puffed the pipe. "I wish we'd not run across that fellow you was with. Tom'd still be alive." She was staring at the wall of the stall beside Kane, her eyes glistening and wet.

"That fellow would still be alive, too," Kane said. "For what it's worth, you took care of him."

"It won't bring back my brother."

"No. But your brother can rest in peace, knowing there was blood vengeance for his murder."

"I miss him."

"I'm sorry. I wish I could have done something to stop him being killed, Miss O'Breen."

"Lordy, don't call me that! I ain't never been called by frilly names."

"Your brother called you Tru. I figured it was short for—" Kane stopped himself short. He'd been about to tell her that he'd assumed that "Tru" was short for Truman, but to say that would reveal that he'd taken her to be a man, which he feared would offend her.

"What was you saying?"

"Just wondering if you want me to call you Tru."

"Call me Trudy. Tru was Tom's name for me. Kind

of just his name to call me, not nobody else. You understand."

"Yes. My name's Kane, by the way. Short for Kanati."

"Cherokee name."

"That's right. 'Lucky Hunter.' "

"Are you lucky?"

"I don't know. I seem to find nothing but trouble everywhere I turn. But I'm still alive despite it. So maybe I am lucky."

She studied him closely, and he wondered what she was thinking.

"Can I ask you something?" he said. "You said you found your brother. How'd you come to be apart?"

"When we was children, we was separated. My father run off from my mother and took Tom with him. Just up and left in the night. He wanted to take me instead of Tom, but I was just a babe, taking milk at our mother's breast at the time, and he couldn't get me. So he took Tom. Tom was my mother's favorite, and she never was happy with me. Wished I was a boy, like Tom, and treated me like I was. I never had no dresses nor hair bows or nothing. It was just as well. With only two of us there, I had to work like a man. My mother always said that to me. 'Trudy O'Breen,' she says, 'You work just like a little man.' "

"Is your mother living?"

"No, no. She died when I was maybe nineteen years old. Died in a fire, one I barely got out of. Breathing in hot smoke made my voice the way it is."

Kane nodded, another question about his new companion answered without his having to ask it.

She continued, "After that I took the notion of finding my father and my brother and set off to do it. I had to track them for years, asking questions, looking under every rock, you might say, until finally I hear word that Mr. Tom O'Breen was working as a policeman in Leavenworth, Kansas. I went and found him. It took some doing to convince him I was his sister. He swore he never knew he had a sister, that our father never said so. And I believe it."

"What about your father?"

"He was dead. I never really saw him, except through the eyes of a baby. I always wished I could have known him. I've spent many an hour thinking about him. Wondering what he looked like, how he'd be just to talk to, all that kind of thing."

Kane was finding that this story struck almost uncomfortably close. "You think you could have forgiven him for leaving you when you were a child?"

She thought about it, then nodded. "Yes. I could have forgiven him. Just to meet him, and to know him . . . that would have meant a lot to me."

"My situation is a lot like yours," Kane said. "I've never seen my father either."

"Tell me about that."

Kane did, sensing in Trudy a receptive and understanding listener, and before he was through, he'd laid out almost his entire story, including his kidnapping by Blessed, the pursuit ever since, his adventures in Dodge City and the mining town of Three Mile, Colorado, his injury and desertion by the train robbers on the Northern Pacific line, and how he'd chanced into the company of Spence, Dominick Jones, and the Rance brothers.

But he told her nothing of the Punjab Star in particular, giving the impression that the "treasure" Blessed sought through him was a stash of old, stolen bank money. And he allowed as well the impression that the pursuit was certainly over and that Blessed was gone, maybe dead.

He would later wonder why he did that and would decide that it was because he sensed in this strange woman a potential good friend and partner. But if she befriended him, he didn't want it to be because she had her eye on an invaluable jewel. And if she abandoned him, he didn't want it to be because she perceived him to be a source of danger. He would conclude all of this in reflections later on, and feel a great sense of guilt. For the moment, he did what he did out of impulse, without analysis or planning.

Trudy listened to his story with wide eyes and an evident fascination, nodding and sometimes giving little grunts and vocalizations at particularly intriguing or exciting portions. When Kane was finished, his tale brought right up to the present moment, she came to her feet as if she'd just heard a rousing speech on a subject that was close to her heart.

"Kane Porterfell, you've found yourself a boon companion in Trudy O'Breen!" she declared. "I never found my own father, but I'll surely help you find yours. And if I've lost one brother, I've surely gained another!" She went over to him, put down her hand to him, and yanked him to his feet. She shook his hand with a broad grin on her face.

"You may not have wanted that Spence fellow to be your partner, but I hope you'll feel different about me," she said. "I'll stick with you and guide you right to the feet of your father, Kane Porterfell. I've done tracking like that before, when I was looking for my own old man, and I can do it again. And I know Helena, too. I was in and about that town for nigh onto two years once. I can show you the lay of the land there. So what do you say? Partners?"

Kane could hardly decline. "Partners," he said, shaking her hand. It was as strong and calloused as that of any man he'd ever known, but even so, it was smaller than a man's hand. As with her general impression, the initial aspect was masculine, but despite it all, traces of her femininity showed through.

"I've got to ask you something," Kane said. "Where'd you learn that fast draw?"

"Taught myself," she said. "I seen a man do it for show once, and I kept working at it until I had it down just right. Want to see?"

Her hand flashed into a blur, and in a moment her pistol was leveled at Kane's forehead, and he was thinking that this had all been a great pretense and show, a way she could toy with him before killing him.

But Trudy only laughed and put the pistol away. "I'll teach you how to do that, if you want. It ain' as hard as it looks, if you'll practice at it."

"Maybe later. Tell me another thing: The men who were left back at the ranch . . . are they dead now?"

"I think so. The one I'd wounded back in Smith-town, he died on his own, without me touching him further. I saw him lying there and knew his face."

"That would have been Mickey Rance. He was the brother of Bub Rance."

"Good riddance, then. If you're going to kill one rat you might as well kill the whole nest. Anyhow, there was another man who come out of the house, and I knife-stuck him. Sneaked up on him, I did, and stung like a scorpion. He died, too, again without me having to do another thing to him. I found him lying on the floor beside the other one."

"The one you knifed was a low-life thief and rob-ber who'd been making plans to rob a train. His name was Dominick Jones."

"To me his name was rubbish if he was the sort to ride with Bub Rance."

"What about the third man? That would be Spence, the one I told you about, who took me in at his line camp. Is he dead too?"

"He put up a good fight, I'll say that for him. We shot back and forth at one another for Lord knows how long. He was fighting scared, though, and that worked against him. He didn't come close to hitting me even once."

"I heard the shots while I was stealing your horse," Kane said.

"Anyway, he managed to get out of the house and head out into the dark, but by then I know I'd shot him at least once. I figure he died out there afterward. I thought I might go look for him, but when I came back to where I'd left my gelding, she was gone. That's when I decided I'd come after you. I recollected seeing you in Smithtown and thinking, 'That there's an Indian.' And I'd seen you spill out the back window of the ranch house, too. If I'd wanted, I could have shot you on the spot."

That gave Kane a chill. She must have moved around toward the rear of the house after stabbing Dominick. He'd not had any idea she was so close when he was making his escape.

"So why didn't you shoot me?"

"Because I always sort of liked Injuns. Always kind of felt like one, the way a lot of people treated me while I was growing up. Like I wasn't as good as everybody else. Like nothing I could ever do would make folks take to me. Like I was just too different from everybody else."

"I know that feeling."

"Anyway, when I found my horse gone, I went back and took one of the horses you and your dead friends had left. I found your track and come here, and you know the rest."

"I appreciate that you didn't kill me," Kane said.

"I probably would have if you hadn't been an Injun. Like I say, I've always sort of liked Injuns."

Kane grinned, but inside he felt like he'd turned to pudding. He'd come close to death several times since his ordeal had begun, but he doubted he'd been any closer, potentially, than he had been while he slept in that stall and Trudy O'Breen stood, armed and with plenty of motivation for vengeance, out in the barn, awaiting the dawn.

Maybe, Kane thought, *my name really does mean something. Maybe I really am a lucky hunter after all.*

Chapter 11

Kane traded horses with Trudy, taking the one she'd commandeered from the corral of the empty ranch house. It was Dominick's old horse, Kane recognized. He cinched the saddle in place and mounted. The chestnut-colored horse was a hand or so smaller than Trudy's, but a strong mount. Spence had commented to Dominick about the quality of the animal while they were riding from the line camp to Smithtown.

"Where to now?" Kane asked.

"Back to that ranch house," Trudy said. "If we're going to ride to Helena, we'll need spare mounts so we can make more miles. I'm sure all your old partners would be glad to let us have the ones they was riding. They sure ain't going to be needing them."

"Maybe we could ride the train," Kane said. "I've got enough money on me for tickets. I'd be happy to pay your fare."

"After all that shooting, and Tom getting killed, I don't think you or me neither one would want to ride no trains, all full of nosy people."

Kane puzzled over what she meant, then comprehended. The shoot-out in Smithtown, with two people killed right there in the tavern, had probably drawn the attention of the territorial marshals by now. Certainly eyewitness accounts would mention that one of those who fled had been a young Indian fellow, and that one of the shooters had been a buck-skinned woman—or would the reports make the same mistake Kane had, and declare Tru a man?

Either way, the law would be watching for people matching Trudy's description and his own.

This was not something Kane needed just now. For the first time he realized that the Smithtown incident might not be fully behind him. And it could poten-tially complicate his purpose in finding his father.

Kane suddenly thought of something that hadn't come to him before. If the Montana Territory law was, or would be, looking for someone matching his description, they'd be looking all the harder for someone matching Trudy's. Kane had been no more than an onlooker in the fight at Smithtown, but Trudy had been an active participant, and whether all the shooting she'd done could be passed off as pure self-defense wasn't something Kane could determine.

If the law began looking for Trudy, she'd be easy to identify. She was nothing if not distinctive. A sharp-eyed lawman could pick her out of a crowd in an instant.

Kane realized it might not be wise to keep com-pany with her after all.

But as he looked her over, watching her readying her horse, he decided the risk was worth it. She was obviously capable and trail-wise, ready to defend herself and her friends. And she'd not killed him when she could have. Further, she was ready to offer help in actually locating Bill Porterfell.

He would stay with her. If there was risk, well, he was used to that. Just now he was glad to have any partner who wasn't Spence.

The body of Dominick still lay dead in the ranch house, Mickey Rance beside him. But of Spence they could find no sign except a bloody trail of tracks leading off onto the plains, toward Smithtown.

"Should we follow them, in case he's out there hurt and needs help?" Kane asked.

Trudy had a huge wad of tobacco jammed in her left jaw and paused to spit before answering. "He ain't hurt out there, believe me. He's dead out there. Look at the amount of blood he's lost. He'd never have made it far on foot with that kind of bleeding going on, and even if he did no more than pass out from the wound, the cold would finish him off." She rolled the chew around in her mouth. "Leave him be. The wolves have to have their food, too."

A rough-edged character, this Trudy Marie O'Breen. But like anyone else, she'd been shaped by the mold of her life experience.

They each took an extra horse, tying the leads off to the horses they rode. They paused to eat some of Trudy's trail food before moving on, Trudy always staying slightly ahead of Kane.

The positioning seemed appropriate. Montana was her territory and her domain, and Kane was glad to have her as a guide.

"We'll need supplies before long," she said. "In fact, before morning. That means we'll have to get them from some rancher or we'll have to find us a store or trading post. Dealing with a rancher would be safest, for word of all the shooting at Smithtown would have been less likely to spread out to individual ranches. But I can't think of a single ranch house in the direction we need to go that ain't too far away to help us just now. But there is a little community with a trading post up six miles to the northwest. So we'll go there. You got money, you say?"

"Yes. Some." Actually, a lot, but Kane saw no need to advertise it.

"Good. Because I got hardly any. Tom always carried the money on him, and I didn't pause to take it off him before I commenced to following you and them you was with. You don't think of such things as money when there's vengeance killing to be done."

Kane was struck by the calm manner in which she talked about the lives she'd taken. He'd heard that in this part of the country, life and death were exceedingly cheap, and justice was less a matter of law than of individual action. Kane, because of his mixed race, was better positioned than most to be wary of stereotypes, but Trudy seemed to be at least some confirmation that there were some who indeed did fill the legendary role of the calm, death-dealing Western plainsman, or in this case, plainswoman.

"Are you certain you can bear not to go back and bury your brother?" Kane asked her.

"The Good Book says to let the dead bury the dead. I knowed him and had his company while he was living, and I can't do naught for him now. Besides, I don't want to go answering a lot of questions for the law. They always come around when there's been shooting and killing."

"That's true."

They rode. The sun came out and the temperature rose. Warmer weather was coming in, and with the added touch of full sunlight, the snow began to melt. The horses stepped along with much greater ease as the snow level declined, and Kane felt downright warm despite the still-frigid air.

"What if there's law at this place we're going?"

"Just a chance we'll have to take."

"I can't afford to be pulled in by the law," Kane said. "If I don't get to Helena soon, I may miss my chance to find my father."

"Ain't no law going to pull you or me in. There's always a way to do what has to be done. We'll just go into that trading post, get what we need, and get out. Actually, I'll do it alone. Indians draw too much attention."

Kane might have pointed out that women in buckskins with voices as raspy and low as a man's also tended to catch the eye. But he didn't want to offend her.

They traveled cross-country, occasionally taking roads and trails, other times making their own. The temperature continued to climb and the snow to decrease. They ate the last of their food and fed the horses the remainder of their grain. Now there truly was no option left but to purchase supplies. Neither they nor the horses would eat again if they didn't.

They passed within sight of a ranch house, where a woman was taking advantage of the unexpected rise in temperature to hang laundry on a clothesline. A big kettle of wash water steamed beside her. She lifted her hand and waved at the two riders, peering at them from beneath the shadowed brim of a big bonnet. Kane and Trudy waved back, knowing they were too far away for their features or clothing to be made out.

A carriage sat in front of the trading post, which was a plain building with sawmill slab siding and a long front porch. From the hidden vantage point of a gully, Kane and Trudy eyed the building and the carriage.

"I don't like the look of that carriage there," Trudy said. "There's a United States marshal in these parts who sometimes rides in a carriage like that. I always thought it odd that a marshal would use such a thing. Seems like something a preacher or lawyer-man ought to use, not a marshal."

"Lots of people have carriages," Kane pointed out. "We don't know that one belongs to the marshal."

"No . . . but it's enough to worry me. Know what else worries me? The way I'm dressed. You don't see all that many folks these days wearing buckskins."

"That's true."

"So if the word has spread this far about the shooting at Smithtown, then the word's probably also spread that one of the people involved had on buckskins."

All these things Kane had thought of before. "I see

your point. But I don't know what we can do about it. You've already said we can't risk me going inside."

Trudy scratched at her chin, thinking. "I think I know what to do," she said. "But it'll require us doubling back for some distance. And we'll have to do a little thieving. Nothing big."

"What do you have in mind?" Kane asked.

She outlined her plan.

Kane was the one who actually pulled off the theft.

It was easier than he anticipated—a quick, furtive sneak, keeping fences and outbuildings and trees between him and the ranch house from which the laundry-hanging woman had waved at them, a swift snatch of a plain blue dress off the clothesline, and a return back the way he'd come.

"Here you are," he told Trudy when he got back to where she awaited him. "I hope it fits you." He grinned. "I feel a little guilty, taking that woman's dress. It's probably one of the few she has."

"Well, she'd be welcome to it as far as I'm concerned," Trudy said, eyeing the garment with distaste. "I've worn a dress only twice before in all my born days. Felt a fool both times."

"You going to put it on now, or later?"

"Later. And I'll wear it only as long as I got to. Come on, let's get away from here before she comes back out to check on her laundry."

She dressed down in the same gully while Kane kept his back turned, though he honestly wasn't sure she would have cared had he watched her. This was no ordinary woman, and he suspected she didn't possess a woman's ordinary scruples and modesty.

"Well, what do you think?" she asked.

Kane turned, and his eyes widened. Though Trudy O'Breen would never be beautiful, the dress did a lot for her. She was a big woman, shoulders as broad as a man's, body built rather squarely—but in the blue dress, and with her hat gone and her hair hanging down, she was indeed a *woman*.

Kane smiled at her. "You look very good, Trudy."

She reddened, looked away, and snorted in mild disdain.

"Come here," he said. "Let me see if I can do anything for you."

She uncomfortably but patiently let him finger-comb her hair and clean the grime from her wide face with a cloth tatter dampened in the little brook that ran through the bottom of the gully.

Kane stepped back and examined his work.

"You're a very handsome woman, Trudy," he said. "You ought to wear a dress more often."

She muttered something quite unladylike in response.

"You think the storekeeper at the trading post will recognize the dress?" he asked.

"I don't know," she said. "I don't plan to stay in there long enough for him to do a lot of thinking about such things."

"Be careful," Kane said. "And don't speak unless you have to. Your voice is recognizable."

"I won't," she said. "I'll be mute as a fence post."

"I suppose, come to think of it, that we should write out what we need, then. That way you can just hand it over to the storekeeper."

Trudy blinked a couple of times and looked away.

"Tell you what . . . why don't you let me write it out?" he said, realizing that she was illiterate.

Trudy finally managed to find some paper in one of her saddlebags. It was an old bill of sale for a box of bullets. Kane had a pencil stub in one of his coat pockets, and he used it to write out the supplies he and Trudy would need to see them through to Helena. He gave her the list and money he'd already taken from the lining of his coat when she wasn't looking. He trusted Trudy as much as he'd trust anyone—but Kane Porterfell had learned never to trust anyone else completely. Except Carolina Railey. Carolina he would trust with his life in any situation, because in his brief time with her, he'd come to know her heart.

"I believe it really would be best for you to do what you said—pretend to be mute," Kane told her. "If anyone asks you to speak, just shake your head and point to your throat."

"All right." She scratched herself in quite masculine fashion, an odd sight indeed now that she was in a dress.

"Be careful," Kane said. "But if you decide you need to get out of there, try not to do it in too big a hurry. That would just rouse suspicions."

"Look here, Injun, if you've got so many thoughts about how to do this, why don't you put on the dress and go in yourself?"

Kane said humbly, "Sorry. I'll shut up."

"You do that." She sighed. "Well, here goes."

Trudy looked about, came up out of the gully, and walked toward the trading post. The carriage was still parked in front of it.

Kane watched her. She paused for a moment at the buggy and glanced inside, looking, Kane knew, for a sign that it belonged to the marshal.

Apparently she found none, for she went on up to the porch, paused a moment—shifting the dress, which obviously felt uncomfortable to her, and gave herself another scratch through the skirt—then went on inside.

Kane sank back down to the bottom of the gully to wait and pray.

Chapter 12

Trudy heard the man's voice even before she stepped inside, and she pegged him for an Easterner right off. She disliked him instantly; she'd met only a few Easterners in her day, but every one of them had offended her.

"So how long have you been in the journalism trade, Mr. Godley?" the storekeeper asked the man as Trudy slipped through the door. She felt the merchant's eyes turn toward her, but she didn't look back at him right away. When she did, he'd turned his attention back to the Easterner, who was seated on a barrel, eating a sandwich.

"Nearly twenty years," the man said, his voice loud and unhesitant—a person accustomed to talking about himself. "I've worked every decent newspaper east of the Mississippi—and a few not so decent—and now I've come to see what journalistic gold I can mine here in the great West."

"I hear there's much interest back East in anything that goes on out here," the storekeeper said.

"Oh, yes," Godley replied around a bite of sandwich. "Indeed. And the more spectacular, the more colorful, the better. What the Easterner wants to believe about the Westerner is that he's always ready for a fight, intelligent but also simple and unsophisticated, and quick with his gun. That's why I was so delighted to hear about what happened at Smithtown. And why I'm in such a rush to get there."

"Rather tragic thing, that," the storekeeper said. He turned away from Godley for a moment. "Ma'am, may I help you?"

Trudy turned and pointed at her list, then at her throat, shaking her head.

"Ah, I see," he said. "Bring me your paper, then. I'll help you out."

Godley took another bite and tipped his hat at Trudy. She could see him eyeing her, could tell that he found her amusing, and hated him all the more for it.

The storekeeper glanced over the list, reading with his lips silently moving, then began taking items off shelves and setting them on the counter.

"Yes," he said, "what happened at Smithtown was tragic, like I said. And not all that common of a kind of event. Yet I understand that the average Easterner believes that there's a shooting a day in your typical Western community." He set a bag of coffee beans on the counter and with his thumbnail put a scratch across that item on the list.

"Well, this is true," Godley said. "And I bear my portion of the blame for that . . . if 'blame' is the right word. What does it matter, after all? Most Easterners will never come west, and you Westerners are so cursed independent that you don't care a whit for the average Easterner's opinion anyway. So why not let him think whatever he wishes to think? Whatever entertains him?"

"You could look at it that way, I suppose. But I do hate for folks elsewhere to consider us uncivilized."

"You must admit, sir, that there's not much of civilization to be seen in the actions of some pistoleer in buckskin blasting away at an entire gang of men in a public tavern."

Trudy had been examining a knife, listening to the men while trying to look as if she weren't. At mention of the "pistoleer in buckskin," she dropped the knife. Self-consciously she hurriedly picked it up and put it back where it had been.

"As I hear the tale, it was one of that gang who fired the first shot and killed the man that the buckskinned one was with," the storekeeper said.

That's right! Trudy said to herself. *It was him that killed my brother! I didn't start nothing . . . but I'm hanged if I didn't finish it!*

Godley brought out a pad of paper and a pencil. "Tell me what you've heard," he said. "Don't worry—I'll attribute nothing to you. Quite honestly, I probably won't even print it. I'm going to Smithtown to get the story right where it happened, after all. But I would like to compare what you tell me to what I find when I get there."

As he continued to busy about, filling Trudy's written supply order, the storekeeper told a version of the events that was, on the whole, accurate. Trudy restrained herself from nodding confirmation of what he said. Godley somehow managed to scribble notes while continuing to eat his sandwich.

Trudy noted with interest that the storekeeper did mention that one of the members of the "gang" who faced down the shootist in buckskin was a young Indian, possibly a half-breed. And she noted with some offense—though not much, because it had happened so often before—that the storekeeper used the word "he" when describing the buckskinned combatant. She was also not happy with his description of the gunman's voice: "Raspy, they say. Like a file on hard metal."

When the storekeeper was finished talking, Godley put away his pad and pencil and ate the penultimate bite of his sandwich.

"Interesting narrative," Godley said. "Though as I've heard the details, you're wrong on several points. The fight, I'm told, was sparked by the one in the buckskins . . . let me see, what can I call him? Ah! The Buckskin Kid. Right! I like it! Anyway, I hear that it was the Buckskin Kid who started the battle and that he was so purely terrifying and unrelenting that he actually ran this desperado gang out of the place, then pursued them across the plains. A few of them went out a window, I hear, including the young Indian."

"I've heard the part about the window, though I'd forgot it," the storekeeper said. "But this 'Buckskin Kid' business . . . you're really going to make up a name like that?"

"I have to call him something, don't I?"

"Where's all this going to be printed?"

"Many places, before it's done. But to begin with, a new newspaper over in Miles City. That's my affiliation of the moment. I've signed on with a typical poor Western editor with no more than a press, a little type, and the hope that he can stir up enough business to keep himself fed."

"Doesn't sound like the kind of business a man can make enough money at to afford fine carriages like what you've got parked out there."

"Oh, the money's not in the local rags. No, no. The money comes from what can be done with the stories *after* they see local print."

"I don't follow you."

"The *Eastern* journals, sir. That's where the money is made! What I publish here I can sell again to the papers and popular magazines back East. It's a simple process, really, but quite effective. Perhaps I shouldn't even be describing the procedure to you, but what the devil!

"It works this way: First you write a 'news' account of an event, under whatever pen name you want to choose, and publish it in one of the local papers. Then you change your hat, so to speak, harvest the very story you planted, and sell it to the Eastern journals. With the story already in printed form in the local paper, it bears more credibility with the Eastern journals."

"Do you mean to tell me you'd make up lies, print them, then point to the fact they're printed as proof that they're true?"

"I try not to *lie*, my friend . . . I do try to get as close to the truth as befits the situation."

"I can't say I much favor your kind of newspapering, friend."

"We do what we must to survive," Godley said dismissively, finishing the sandwich. "And along the way, we entertain who we can. I thank you, my friend, for the food and the conversation."

The storekeeper grunted at Godley, then turned to Trudy and said, "Ma'am, I think this is all you asked for, except the horse feed. There's some bags of that there on the floor, and I'll carry that out for you."

Trudy shook her head, went over, bent down, and picked up two sacks of feed as if they were filled with pillow down. Both the storekeeper and the journalist were impressed. Godley yanked out his pad and scribbled a quick note.

Trudy laid the feed sacks on the counter and handed the money to the storekeeper. He opened his cashbox and began counting out change.

Godley tipped his hat to her again. "A pleasure to meet a strong Western woman," he said, smiling cattishly. Trudy eyed him sidewise and pondered the offensiveness and absolute uselessness of anything that came from the far side of the Mississippi.

The storekeeper must have felt similarly, because he said to Godley, "You'll be moving on now, I suppose. Eager to get to Smithtown."

"In a few minutes," Godley said, sitting back to pick at his teeth with a small silver toothpick attached to his watch chain.

The storekeeper bundled the flour, coffee, and other such supplies that Trudy had ordered in brown paper and tied it all up with twine. He made a long loop so she could carry it across her shoulder.

"You sure you don't want help with that feed?" he asked.

Trudy answered by slinging the bundle over her left shoulder and picking up the feed sacks, one per shoulder. She turned and headed out the door, the storekeeper and the irksome journalist watching.

She was just outside the door when she heard Godley say, "There goes the ugliest woman I do believe I've ever seen."

She'd have considered killing him if she hadn't been in such a hurry and if she'd had her weapons on her. She comforted herself with the knowledge that it would have been a waste of a perfectly good bullet anyway.

Kane greeted her with relief.

"That took longer than I'd thought," he said. "I was afraid something was going wrong."

"No. Nothing wrong."

"No marshal inside?"

"No. That carriage belongs to some bigmouth Eastern fellow. Not the marshal."

"Did they act odd toward you?"

She glared at him, still burning from the parting insult she'd overheard Godley make toward her, and Kane knew he'd offended her.

"Why would they have acted odd?" she huffed.

"No reason. I'm sorry. Well, I suppose we should move on now."

"Not until I'm out of this dress."

"Don't you think we should get farther on before you change?"

She was already yanking at it, though, and Kane turned his back and waited. "You can turn around now," she said after a brief time.

She was her old, masculinized self again. The dress was in a heap on the ground.

"Let's take that with us," Kane said. "We might need it again."

"You take it if you want. I don't want it."

Kane did take it, rolling it up and putting it in one of his saddlebags. They packed away the supplies and lashed the big sacks of feed behind them on the back rises of their saddles.

"Let's go," Trudy said, still grouchy.

"Wait," said Kane as she spurred her horse up out of the gully. "Let's go down so they don't see us from the trading post."

It was too late. Trudy was already coming into view. Kane sighed and followed, supposing it wouldn't really matter.

At that moment Godley came out onto the porch, still picking his teeth, and paused when he saw Trudy. He looked her up and down, his eyes widening.

"The Buckskin Kid!" he declared softly, but loud enough that she heard him.

"You need to learn to close that big mouth of yours," Trudy rasped at him. "Someday somebody'll decide to close it for you for good."

Godley backed away, gaping now, finding in the odd, grating rasp of the voice further confirmation that this person, whom he'd seen only minutes before in the form of a woman, was indeed the very Smithtown gunman he'd just tagged "The Buckskin Kid."

"Dear Lord above!" he exclaimed, his own voice quite high in the excitement of realization. "Mother of . . . it really *is* you!"

Kane then appeared, rising like a mounted phantom out of the deep gully, and Godley stared at him as well, growing even more visibly agitated.

"Come on," Kane urged Trudy, who was sitting her horse in statuesque stillness, glaring at Godley, thinking about killing him. Obviously something more had gone on in the trading post than Trudy had told him. "Let's get on out of here!"

Trudy stared at Godley a moment longer, turned away, and whipped her horse into a run. Kane followed, a little more slowly, for the two spare horses were trailing his and weren't eager to run.

The storekeeper emerged.

"What's going on here?" he asked the still-astonished Godley.

"That man . . . that woman . . . whatever he, she is . . . that was the Buckskin Kid!"

"What?" He looked at the figures of Kane and Trudy, quickly growing small in the distance. "You're sure?"

"Yes! Yes! He was in buckskin, he had the voice, just as you described . . . and he pointed at me, threatened me! It was the woman, the same one who was inside just now! But it wasn't really a woman. It's a man!"

The storekeeper laughed. "My friend, the Western air has driven you loco. That absolutely was not a man in my store!"

"It was! It was the Buckskin Kid—and there was a young Indian man with him! Just as you described!"

"The story as I heard it was that the Indian was in the gang she was shooting at. He wasn't with your Buckskin Kid but against him."

"Well, maybe you heard the story wrong. Or maybe he's taken him prisoner. Or maybe it's an entirely different Indian. But one thing is sure: The Buckskin Kid has a young Indian man riding with him now."

"I'm telling you again, Mr. Godley: The woman in the store was a true woman. Not a man. She was ugly, that's true, but she was certainly a woman."

"How can you be sure? She might have been a man in a woman's dress and wig. The Buckskin Kid in disguise!"

The storekeeper paused and looked embarrassed. "Because as she bent to pick up those feed sacks, the top of her dress drooped down. That's how I know. I wasn't *trying* to look, mind you. It just happened."

Godley frowned. "You're certain?"

"I'm certain."

He pondered that. "It can only mean one thing, then. The Buckskin Kid is a woman." He scratched at his whiskers, thoughtful. "I'll need a different name now. The Buckskin . . . Belle! Aha! That's it! Absolutely musical! The Buckskin Belle!" Godley was suddenly bouyant; he reached over and took the storekeeper's hand, pumping it vigorously.

"I thank you, sir. This is surely the most productive time I've spent as a journalist! What a story I have to print now! The Buckskin Belle, murderess of the Montana Territory—riding in the clothes of a man and the company of a fearsome Indian warrior! What a story!"

He fairly ran to his buggy, leaped into the seat, threw the brake, and rumbled away.

The storekeeper watched him, shook his head, and went back inside.

God save us from Eastern fools, he thought. *Especially those with access to printing presses.*

Chapter 13

Miles City, Montana Territory, a few days later

A subtle but decided limp marked the broadly built man's gait as he crossed the dirt street toward a three-story hotel that had already received his close, and disapproving, scrutiny. Even so, he strode toward it; there was no better place to be had.

He was weary, many miles behind him and many more to go. He'd always despised the railroad—its long, rumbling, dull stretches in which a man was vibrated and jarred and smoked like a ham in a shed— but choices in travel were like choices in hotels. A man selected the best available and made do with it.

He shifted his leather valise from one hand to the other, hefted his sizable but strong form up onto the hotel porch, took one more unhappy glance up and down this wretch of a town, and put his hand on the doorknob.

His mood did not improve once he was inside. Immediately he pegged the young desk clerk for what he quickly verified he was: over-eager, over-friendly, and over-inquisitive.

"Well, sir, come in! Pleased to have you visit Miles House."

"I can't imagine what you're finding to smile at."

The young man's grin faltered, then he cranked it up again and chuckled. "Right, sir. Can I help you?"

"You can tell me if you have a godforsaken room in which I can spend a godforsaken night in this godforsaken town."

The clerk was seeming more uncertain and younger by the moment. The grin failed to survive this time, despite a valiant effort.

"We have some rooms, yes."

"Then how about you sign me up for whichever one is the least miserable, hmmm?"

"Yes, sir."

The young man fumbled about beneath the desk. "Blast it . . . sorry, sir . . . I seem to be having trouble finding the key."

The man sighed loudly.

"It's our best room, too . . . a fine view."

The man rolled his eyes. "View of what? I can't imagine anything worth seeing here."

Still looking for the key, the clerk struggled to fill the gap with conversation. "So . . . what brings you to Miles City, sir?"

"The railroad. And business that's entirely my own."

The clerk failed to take the hint. "A businessman, are you?"

The man grunted softly, ready to let the conversation die.

"Most business in Miles City involves cattle. Are you a cattleman?"

"No. Listen, son, I'll take any room, if you find the key for it."

"Let me look right here, sir . . . ah! Yes!" Triumphant, the clerk stood, key in hand and grin back on his face.

"Congratulations," the man said in a tone of weary sarcasm.

"That's room B-2. As I said, a fine view. So, sir, how long will you be with us?"

"One night. I'm going to Helena."

"Beautiful city, Helena."

"You know Helena, do you?"

"Well . . . I've never actually been there, but I'm told it's lovely."

"Right now a hot supper and a soft bed sound lovely to me."

"We'll get you signed right in, sir." The clerk grabbed the guest register. "Your name?"

"Blessed. Robert Blessed."

"Blessed. Yes, sir. Robert Blessed."

"Tell me, young man, where can a man find a good supper in this town?"

The clerk crinkled his brow, recommended a café, and handed Blessed the key to his room. Blessed was just about to muster up the grace to say a thank-you when the lobby door burst open and a small boy, laden with newspapers, entered with a grand flourish.

"Free copy of the *Miles City Argus*, sir?" he asked,

waving one at Blessed. "Not a cent's charge for the best news in all the Montana Territory!"

"Get out of here with that rag!" the clerk said. "You know you're not supposed to come busting in here, bothering our guests!"

The boy would not be deterred. "Never mind him, sir—he just wants that you shouldn't get to read about all the big news of the Territory—the big cattle freeze, the fire over at Timber Creek, and the big shoot-out between the Buckskin Belle and the desperadoes at Smithtown."

"Out of here!" the clerk demanded, pointing at the door.

"Wait a minute there, son . . . Did you say that newspaper is free?"

"Yes, sir. Free editions for the first two months, just so folks will see how great a newspaper it is. Then everybody will want to buy a subscription."

"Clever arrangement. Here, let me have one. I like to read before I sleep."

The boy gave Blessed a newspaper and shot the clerk a victorious look.

Now that Blessed had his key and some reading material, he was in a better mood. "So, who's the Buckskin Belle?" he asked the news vendor.

"Just the meanest, shootingest female desperado there is," the boy said. "Killed a bunch of men over at Smithtown a few days ago. Ain't nobody caught her yet, neither." He fell into a singsong recitation that Blessed would later find came directly from the newspaper account. "She rides the Territory in the company of her faithful Indian companion, striking fear into every criminal heart, her guns ready and her eye keen . . ."

Blessed glanced at the clerk. "This is, I suppose, a joke of some sort."

"No," the clerk admitted. "There really was a shoot-out. And one of the people involved was a man in buckskin clothes. For some reason, our new local paper has decided that this man was really a woman dressed like a man, and they're calling her the 'Buckskin Belle.' If you ask me, it probably was a man all along, and they're just trying to drum up interest in their paper."

"Nothing wrong with that," Blessed said. He picked up his bag and headed for the stairs. At the base of the staircase he paused. "Is there really an Indian companion for this Buckskin Belle?"

"I think so, sir," the clerk said. "At least, the paper claims there is. Other versions of the story say the Indian was one of the ones being shot at. And that he might have been a half-breed, not a full Indian."

Blessed's eyes narrowed. "Half-breed?"

"That's what some say."

Blessed stared at the floor a moment, then turned and walked up the stairs without further words.

Blessed didn't bother to read the story prior to his supper, and in fact he forgot about the newspaper completely as he dined. The café was decent as Western small-town cafés went, and he ate slowly and enjoyed three cups of coffee after the food was gone.

He was a tired man, and if he allowed himself to admit it, a discouraged one. Pondering the fact that he was in Miles City, Montana Territory, and still not in possession of the jewel that he wanted more than anything else in existence, filled him with astonishment.

It all should have gone so easily. He and his partner, Jason Wyrick, had used money and muscle to obtain copies of the mysterious coded letters that went out to a handful of former members of the late war's infamous rebel guerrilla band, Patrick's Raiders. But one letter, the one in possession of Bill Porterfell, he'd been unable to obtain, and this despite hiring some of the hardest, meanest ruffians available. Finally, in desperation, he'd kidnapped the half-Cherokee son of Bill Porterfell . . . only to have the unexpectedly clever young man escape from him, steal his letters—and memorize and destroy the blasted things!—then lead him on a wild and deadly chase across the West.

Along the way, men had died. And his partner, Jason Wyrick, had been blinded by Kane himself.

Blessed repeated to himself a pledge he'd made privately many times before: When all this was done and the Punjab Star was in his hands, Kane Porterfell would die. That pleasure would, to Blessed, be almost as great as owning the fabled blue diamond.

In Colorado he'd come so close, so tantalizingly *close*—only to have the greed of a wealthy mine magnate ruin his chance.

He'd lost Kane's trail after that, and it had taken him too long to figure out how to pick it up again. Once he did, it was easy: a few questions to agents at the rail station, a few dollars slipped into a few pockets, and he'd easily learned that the cursed half-breed was headed for Helena, Montana Territory.

And now so was Robert Blessed. Where Kane went, Blessed would follow.

Blessed could think of only one reason Kane would go to Helena: William Porterfell must be there.

That worried Blessed to some degree. Kane had a strong lead on him. By now he had probably united with his father in Helena. They'd probably pooled their knowledge, re-created and decoded the letters, and maybe even put their hands on the Punjab Star.

Blessed hoped not. Without that diamond, he had no chance of regaining the wealth that the years had taken from him. And he surely had no ambition to die a penniless and broken man.

Blessed finished his meal and left money on the table. He stepped out into the brisk Miles City evening and took a stroll about town, thinking how deeply he despised the far West. He'd grown up in the East and had spent most of his postwar years no farther west than Missouri. If it had been up to him, he'd never have gone beyond that.

But for that diamond, he would go as far as need be. Right to the very edge of the Pacific Ocean. For that matter, right to the very edge of hell.

He lit a cigar, puffing on it as he headed back to his hotel. Climbing the stairs to his room, he finished his smoke and began to think about sleep. He would just relax, read that newspaper, and get some badly needed rest.

He entered the room and locked the door behind him.

* * *

Blessed did not sleep much that night. Two things he found in the newspaper kept him from it.

One was the account of the shoot-out at Smithtown, a community, he gathered, that was some miles ahead up the railroad. The story told of the involvement of a young Indian, possibly a half-breed, in the incident. Though it had appeared at the time, according to witnesses, that this young man was a part of the party who had suffered the vengeance of the "Buckskin Belle," there was a possibility, the story implied, that he might actually have been in league with her, in that he was clearly seen by the reporter himself riding in the company of the woman outlaw.

Blessed knew that it was foolish to assume this young Indian was Kane. Why should it be he? Kane was bound for Helena. Why would he have stopped short of that to involve himself with some pants-wearing female shootist? The West was full of young Indians and half-breeds. Why assume this one was Kane?

Yet Blessed couldn't shake off the conviction that it might be Kane. And, ironically, a second item in the newspaper gave him grounds for at least the possibility that his intuition might be correct.

This story, older and played much lower in the rather luridly styled paper, described a train robbery that had occurred right about the time that Kane would have been traveling toward Helena, Blessed had calculated.

The robbers had stopped the train and raided passenger baggage, jewelry, purses, and the like as usual . . . but something else had happened as well. There had been a fight between some of the robbers and a young Indian man, and witnesses had said the robbers had beaten this young Indian and hauled him off into the plains north of the tracks, no doubt to kill him there.

The possibility that Kane was this young Indian, and that he now was dead, intrigued and horrified Blessed, though only because a dead Kane meant that the letters, which had existed only in Kane's mind, would now be irretrievable and all would be lost.

But what if this young Indian, assuming it was Kane, hadn't died? What if, perhaps, this renegade woman in buckskin had saved him?

Well after midnight, after hours of such speculation, Blessed suddenly laughed. How absurd he was being! Almost certainly neither the Indian victimized in the train robbery nor the one—if he existed—who rode with this "Buckskin Belle" was Kane Porterfell.

But the possibility was there—and as long as it was, doubt and questions would linger.

Fortunately, the newspaper account of the Smithtown incident provided a particular piece of information that might lead to an answer. And with Smithtown just up the track, it would be relatively easy to make his inquiry. He expected to find no more than a confirmation that Kane was uninvolved in either of the situations about which he'd just read—but at least he would know.

A man involved in the shooting, a fellow identified as one Jim Spence, had been found staggering toward

Smithtown, wounded and covered in clotting, freezing blood, about dawn the day after the Smithtown shoot-out. By this time a territorial marshal had been summoned to investigate the incident, and he promptly took this fellow prisoner.

But Spence wasn't locked up yet. His wound had been treated, according to the story, and he was now lodged temporarily, under hired guard, in a room in a Smithtown house, there to remain until he was healed enough to be taken to more official quarters for a thorough questioning, not just about the shooting but about past crimes that he had allegedly done farther east.

Blessed found the idea of making a call on Spence to be worthwhile. He would ask a few questions, satisfy himself that Kane wasn't involved, and move on to Helena.

That decided, Blessed turned on his side, stared for a few moments into the darkness, then closed his eyes and began to snore.

Chapter 14

Smithtown, Montana Territory

Joey Deward leaned back in his chair and studied with pride the document in his hand. It was maybe the hundredth time he'd perused it since it had been given him, but still it enthralled him. Nobody had ever entrusted him to do any kind of important job until now. Folks had tended to laugh at him behind his back, call him simple and foolish.

This quickly scribbled document, signed by an authentic United States territorial marshal, showed them wrong. Joey Deward was *deputized.* Put in charge of guarding the wounded man named Spence until the marshal got back from wherever it was he'd gone. Nobody could laugh at that kind of duty or call it the job of a fool!

Deward smiled in satisfaction at the paper, folded it, and put it in his pocket. He glanced up at the man on the bed.

Spence was staring at him, eyes rather blank because of the stupefying medicine that Deward kept feeding him, as the marshal had ordered, but still lively enough to let his contempt show through.

"Think that paper's mighty fine, don't you, boy?" Spence said, his voice a low slur.

"I don't want to talk to you," Deward said, reaching to the floor beside him and picking up a crumpled newspaper that he'd perused almost as thoroughly as his deputizing paper.

" 'Don't want to talk to you,' " Spence repeated, trying but failing to mimic Deward's voice. " 'Don't want to talk to you.' "

Deward examined the newspaper, a copy of the new one being printed over in Miles City. He was a slow reader, picking words apart letter by letter and putting them together again, sometimes correctly, sometimes not, but this story interested him enough to make it worth the effort.

It was the lurid recounting of the shooting in which Spence himself had been a participant, though Spence had told him several times that he personally never fired a shot, never really had anything to do with the events that started the fight in the first place, and had never desired to find trouble with the "Buckskin Belle" even after she trailed them all to that deserted ranch. All he'd done was defend himself, he swore.

Deward read the familiar newspaper account again, his lips moving with each word. Spence watched him with an annoyed grimace, then rolled slowly on the bed, seeking a comfortable position.

Deward lowered the newspaper. "You'd better

quit rolling around like that," he said. "You'll tear that bullet hole open again."

"Shut up. Go back and read your deputizing paper, you aggravating half-wit."

"I ain't no half-wit. I may not be the smartest man ever walked, but I'm no half-wit!"

Spence had learned early on that he could get on Deward's nerves by disparaging him that way, and he took delight in doing it at every chance. Those chances weren't all that many, though. The marshal had ordered that Spence be kept thoroughly doped up so he wouldn't try to escape, and so he spent most of his time asleep.

He'd come to hate that dope and love it at the same time. It gave him the most wonderful, deep sleeps, but the taste was awful, and the way his head felt after he woke up was sickening.

Spence turned, felt a stab of opiate-numbed pain, and winced. He tried to wriggle the fingers of his left hand but had little luck. He wondered if it was because of the frostbite or the bandaging. The latter, he hoped. He'd hate to see his fingers fall away like a leper's.

Deward put down the newspaper at last, got out of his chair, and walked to Spence's bedside.

"I still can't figure out why you fellows was so stupid as to go up against the Buckskin Belle," Deward said.

Spence reddened with exasperation and anger. "You blasted, dim-witted, babbling fool!" he said. "How many times have I got to tell you? We didn't know who she was at the time. There never was a

'Buckskin Belle' until that newspaper made up the name! And I ain't convinced even yet that it was a woman at all. If she was, she shot as well as any man I've ever seen. Now get back in your chair and leave a man in peace!"

"You need more medicine," Deward said.

"No, no! I'm sick of that stuff! You're going to kill me with it, as much as you pour down me! Where do you think I'm going to run off to, anyway? I've got a damned bullet hole in my side!"

"Yeah, but not bad enough to kill you. The doctor said that, remember? Said your wound was bad because it bled a lot, but not in any other way. Didn't touch nothing vital."

"Leave me alone. I swear, if I have to spend much more time with you, you babbler, I'd as soon go ahead and die."

"I'll get you some more medicine."

Spence swore and cursed and tried to get up, but Deward had this routine down cold and, as usual, Spence came out the loser. Deward pinned him expertly, held his head down just so with his elbow, pinched Spence's nose shut to force his mouth open, and poured a sizable dose of the syrupy opiate down Spence's throat.

Spence blubbered and fell back limply, eyes squeezed shut, lips smacking miserably in reaction to the bitter medicine.

"It ain't right that this can be done to an innocent man in a free country," he complained. "It ain't right at all."

Deward corked the bottle, then held it up critically to examine its level.

"You're going to kill me with that stuff," Spence muttered weakly.

"No. I'm careful. I don't give no more than they said I could. It'd take a lot more than what I give to kill you."

"Ain't right . . ." Spence was already starting to sound slower, duller, the drug beginning its work.

There was a sharp rap on the door of the room, startling both men inside. Deward almost dropped the bottle.

He went to the door, opened it, and found himself looking at a distinguished-appearing, gray-bearded man with a broad face and an intense manner.

"What can I do for you?" Deward asked.

"And who might you be?" the man asked in turn, very authoritatively.

"My name's Deward. I'm deputized by the territorial marshal, and I'm on duty guarding my prisoner. Are you wanting in?"

"I'm here to see that prisoner. I'm a doctor."

"Oh! But why'd you come? Doc Morris has already looked him over."

The gray-bearded man frowned deeply. "It's Doc Morris who asked me to see him. Now, if you'll step aside and let me in . . ."

"Well . . . I guess that's all right." Deward sidestepped uncertainly, and the big man swept in past him.

"Now, Mr. Deward, you may leave the room a few minutes. Go take a walk. Get some fresh air."

"I don't know as I should leave."

"For heaven's sake, man, I'm not going to let your prisoner go anywhere. And I do insist on the right to examine him privately."

"Well . . . all right." Deward took the bottle to the shelf and set it there.

"What's that in the bottle?" the intimidating man asked. "Are you drinking on the job?"

"No! That's not for me. It's medicine, for him." He pointed at Spence, who was taking all this in through drooping, half-shut eyes. "The doctor gave it to him for pain, and the marshal's having me use it to keep him sleeping, so he won't run off."

"Where's the marshal?"

"He had to go back to Miles City on business. He'll be in tomorrow to take charge of Mr. Spence there."

"I see. You may go now."

Cowed and no longer feeling in charge, Deward nodded obediently, took his hat off a wall peg, and left the room. The gray-bearded man listened as Deward's footsteps faded away, and he heard a door open and close.

"What kind of doc are you?" Spence asked, sounding like his tongue was as thick as his forearm.

"Rather unusual way to keep a man hog-tied, that I must say," the bearded man replied. "I have to hand it to the marshal for his cleverness, in any case."

"Who are you?"

"I'm not a doctor, that I can tell you. I'm a man needing nothing more than information. You were

144

involved in the shooting incident here in this sorry little backwater, am I right?''

"You some newspaperman or something?"

"Just a private citizen. No one who can do you any harm. What I'm wanting to know about, specifically, is something I read in the newspaper. A young Indian who was involved in some way in the shoot-out."

Despite Spence's steady descent toward a drug-induced sleep, that question sparked a little bit of life in his eyes. "Who are you?" he asked.

"Does it matter? All I'm wanting is confirmation that the Indian fellow was not a young half-breed by the name of Kanati Porterfell. Goes by Kane, usually . . ."

Spence reacted to the name rather startlingly. "Kane . . . wait a minute. Wait a minute! You're the man he said has chased him . . . you're Robert Blessed!"

Blessed was taken aback. "Good Lord, man . . . it *was* Kane?"

Spence raised his bandaged and frostbitten hand in an attempt to point. The drug was taking fuller effect by the moment, stripping from him all pretense and craftiness. He was at this moment incapable of subtlety or falsehood. "You stay away from Kane! That diamond's going to be mine! *Mine!*"

Blessed's eyes narrowed. "So Kane's been talking, has he? Just how much do you know, Mr. Spence?"

"I know you've chased him for mile upon mile. I know you've killed men! I know you're after that

Punjab Star! But you can't have it! Kane's *my* partner now!"

Blessed stared at Spence for a few moments. "I'm very sorry you're so knowledgeable. Too much knowledge can be dangerous to a man."

"I'll have the law on you! I'll tell the law about . . . how you murdered Kane's mother . . . and all the bad things you done . . . while you were chasing Kane . . ." Spence was wavering, about to pass out.

"Where is Kane now, Mr. Spence?"

"Not here . . . not here . . . still looking for his pap. But I'll . . . catch up to him . . . once I get out of my situation here . . . and go on to . . ."

"To Helena? Is that where he's gone?"

"Don't know where he is . . . I know Helena was where . . . we was headed when we had the trouble . . . in the . . . tavern . . ."

Spence's body seemed to grow heavier and sink deeply into the bed. His mouth fell open and his eyes closed.

"Mr. Spence?"

His only answer was a low moan.

"I see," Blessed said. "Conversation's over."

He stood rubbing his chin and thinking hard. This man on the bed was a potential problem. Once interrogated by the law, he'd probably tell everything he knew, and obviously Kane had told him much, had named names. Robert Blessed didn't need that kind of trouble.

Fortunately, an answer was easily at hand. Blessed had spotted the dim-wittedness of that so-called deputy the moment he'd laid eyes on him. It was remarkable that such a foolish fellow had been left with a responsibility as potentially dangerous as administering an opiate to an already overmedicated man. A little too much overdoing of that job could lose a man his prisoner.

Blessed retrieved the bottle that Deward had placed on the shelf. Still about half full. Plenty to do the job.

Blessed uncorked it, sniffed it, and made a face. He paused to lock the door but found the lock unfunctional. No matter. This would only take a moment.

He went over to Spence, tilted the sleeping man's head back and propped the mouth open, and poured slowly, holding Spence's head up a little and giving him plenty of time to swallow reflexively. Bit by bit the contents of the bottle receded until it was empty.

Robert Blessed stood, recorked the empty bottle, and smiled.

Spence was going to have a very long sleep indeed. No one could survive the dosage he'd just received.

Blessed took the bottle back to the shelf and was setting it in place when the door opened. Deward was there. Blessed wheeled, surprised. The fool must have crept back softly, for he'd heard no footsteps.

"Look here, doctor," Deward said. "I been thinking. I probably shouldn't have left you here alone with him. I mean, it's my job to keep watch." Deward paused. "What were you doing with that medicine bottle?"

"Examining it, sir," Blessed said, recovering

quickly from his surprise. "I think you've been overdosing the patient."

"I been giving just the amount I was told, to keep him in that bed."

"In that case, we have nothing to worry about. Good day." Blessed headed for the door.

Deward stepped aside. "But wait, doctor. I want to ask you about—"

"Good day," Blessed said again and headed out the opposite door and was gone.

Deward stood there, frowning. Something about the incident that just transpired was strange and unnerving.

Something was wrong.

He went to Spence's bedside. The man was deeply asleep, mouth open, tongue lying to one side against his teeth. His eyes were open in slits, dull orbs barely visible.

He was breathing slowly. More slowly than ever before. It made Deward want to gasp for breath to see how little air the man was taking in.

Walking across the room, he picked up the bottle, and was jolted with shock. Empty! But he knew he'd left it half full. He'd been carefully monitoring every dose he put into Spence, like Doc Morris and the marshal both had firmly instructed him.

That doctor . . . if a doctor he was . . . must have poured the rest of the contents into Spence! Why? Was he trying to kill the man?

Deward stood there frozen, bottle in hand, and didn't know what to do. He vaguely realized that if

Spence died, the blame might fall on him. Had any-one else even seen that doctor fellow? Would they accuse him of having made the man up to cover his own guilt?

Spence simply couldn't be allowed to die. He had to find some way to stop that from happening.

Deward put the bottle back on the shelf, but too hurriedly. It fell and smashed on the floor. By the time it hit, though, Deward was already halfway across the room, headed back to Spence's bedside.

He hesitated only a moment, then rolled the nearly unbreathing Spence onto his side. It was like rolling a dead man. Taking a deep breath, Deward made a face, jammed two fingers back into Spence's open mouth, and pressed them against the back of his throat.

Spence gagged heavily. Deward kept pressing.

In moments, Spence heaved. The contents of his stomach came up, and Deward saw clear evidence of the amount of medicine that had been poured into the man—far more than Deward had administered.

When Spence had heaved himself empty, Deward rose, wiped his fouled hand on the sheet, and went in search of rags. He would clean the mess up, attri-bute the vomiting to the medicine, and dispose of the bottle, claiming he'd dropped it by accident and sopped up the spilled contents.

Then he would pray very hard that Spence would live and that the marshal would get back very soon.

Joey Deward didn't want to be a deputy anymore.

* * *

Robert Blessed's original intention had been to come to Smithtown on the train, but some instinct had made him change his plans. Under a false name, he'd rented a horse and saddle from a rancher, pledging to return both within forty-eight hours, and ridden to Smithtown on horseback.

He was glad he'd followed that instinct. Though he hadn't come here planning to kill anyone, now that he had, he certainly couldn't afford to be loitering about town waiting for the next train.

He rode out of Smithtown slowly, not wanting to attract attention, but once out of view he ran the horse mercilessly, putting the town behind him. He rested the horse briefly when it had gone as long as it could, then ran it some more. Only when he felt relatively safe did he let it rest and feed.

He made the next train station by evening. The horse he simply unsaddled and turned loose; the saddle he dumped near the railroad tracks for whoever might find it.

Heart pounding, fearing that the law might be upon him because of Spence's death, for surely the man was long dead by now, Blessed purchased a railroad ticket under a second false name. To his good fortune, the next train was due in at noon. He spent the morning smoking cigars and pretending to read a newspaper. When he got aboard the train there were no stares, no lawmen, no undue questions. Just a smile and ticket punch from the conductor, and he was on his way.

Blessed relaxed. He was bound for Helena again, and by disposing of Spence he had put a potential problem behind him almost before it presented itself.

For a few moments, his brightest hopes seemed real. He really was going to find Kane, and Kane's father, and in the end, they really would lead him to the Punjab Star.

Exactly how it would all work out he didn't know, but somehow it was all going to happen. He could just feel it.

Chapter 15

Kane, weary, muddy, and numb from the cold, rode slowly into the town of Helena at the side of Trudy O'Breen and thought about how happy he should be finally to be here, how excited, how anticipatory of at last finding his father.

He felt none of those things. In fact, he felt almost nothing at all. The physical and mental stress of travel, compounded by the still-healing injury to his skull and the weakening effects of the fever he'd only recently shaken off, had rendered him almost without emotion.

The only thing that could stir much passion in him right now was the thought of a warm, dry room and a soft, clean, comfortable bed.

It was midday, though a heavily overcast sky made it seem later. Snow was falling, but half-heartedly, just a few flakes peppering down, dodging here and there in the shifting wind before finally deciding where they would land.

"Here we are, Kane," Trudy O'Breen said with a tone of satisfaction. "I told you we'd make it safe."

"I do appreciate all your help and friendship,"

Kane said, and he meant it. Trudy had gone from being a feared, phantomlike, vengeful enemy to being a true and devoted companion and protector. Had he viewed this situation from the outside, Kane might have suspected that Trudy, despite her generally masculine outlook on life and the fact that she was several years his senior, harbored some romantic attraction toward him. Being on the inside of the situation, though, he knew this wasn't true. She was simply a person with a remarkable capacity for friendship, and by a simple act of will she had decided that Kane would be her friend.

Trudy slumped in the saddle, slogging through the rather muddy center of the street. She looked to the right and left. "Town's changed some since I was here," she said. "Looks better, really. More paint. Lot of newer buildings."

The boardwalks and the streets themselves were full of people, busying about . . . but not fully minding their own business, Kane noticed. Many of them were staring openly at him and Trudy.

He was struck with a very uncomfortable feeling of déjà vu. This very thing had happened to him before, when he rode into Dodge City in the company of Frederick and Carolina Railey. People had gaped at him, followed him, whispered about him, and put the law on his tail—and he'd wound up jailed simply because he bore a resemblance to an Indian outlaw who had victimized a few Kansans of the vicinity.

Not again! he thought, as more glances and outright stares came his way.

So far Trudy hadn't seemed to notice. "You know, Kane, now that we're here, we got some thinking to do. There's a lot of folks in this town, and it ain't going to be easy to find your pap."

"I know," Kane replied. "I've been thinking about that . . . though not much. Mostly I've just had my thoughts fixed on getting here."

"First thing we need to do is eat and find some lodgings and somewhere to stable the horses."

"I agree. I'm empty." Kane paused. "Trudy . . ."

"I've already noticed," she cut in. "Folks staring at us."

"I've seen a few whispering to one another, too," Kane pointed out.

"I've been known to draw a few looks in my time," Trudy said. "Most womenfolk don't look like me. But this is more than that, I think."

"Because I'm an Indian, you think?"

"These folks have seen plenty of Indians before."

"I don't like this, Trudy. This same kind of thing happened to me before in Kansas, and I wound up in a jail cell accused of somebody else's crimes."

"Let's get off the street," Trudy said. "I don't like it, neither."

Hungry, they tied the horses off to a hitching post outside a rough-hewn café that spilled lots of smoke and mouthwatering aromas. As they walked into it together, three men watched closely from a nearby porch, turning their heads and looking a bit pallid all at once when Trudy turned and stared back at them.

Kane commented on that. "Trudy, judging from what those men just did, I'd take a guess that it might be you, instead of me, who's drawing the attention."

"Maybe so," she said. "But I don't know why. I ain't famous."

They went inside and found a table at a back corner. Several people in the place gave them peculiar, lingering looks, and others seemed afraid to look at them at all except out of the corners of their eyes.

The waiter seemed nervous, too. They ordered steaks, potatoes, and coffee. He took the order mentally, nodded quickly, and hustled away from them as if they were diseased. Kane noticed that the waiter whispered something to the man at the bar as soon as he got there, and both quickly glanced at their table, then looked away fast when they saw that Kane had his eye on them.

The food arrived at last, and Kane and Trudy set into it with enthusiasm. They were both so hungry that for the duration of the meal, they hardly noticed the attention they were getting and didn't talk at all.

When Kane was satisfied at last, he leaned back, wiped his mouth with a napkin, and said, "Let's talk, Trudy. Tell me how I can find my father."

"Maybe he's one of them who's staring at us. Or maybe he's put out word of who he's looking for, and folks recognize that's who you are."

This suggestion excited Kane for a few moments, until he realized that if it were correct, it would be he, rather than Trudy, who was drawing most of the attention.

"Well, I can't explain the stares," Kane said. "I also can't presume it has anything to do with my search

for my father. I'm not going to wait for him to come
to me. I have to figure out a way to actually find
him."

"Somebody's coming," Trudy muttered under
her breath.

Kane looked up and saw a slender, dark-haired,
pale-faced man heading toward them from the bar.
He was smiling and nodding, rather like a very old
man, though he wasn't, and shuffling slowly, as if to
avoid even the remotest chance of startling them.

Kane didn't know whether to stand and ready
himself to fight, or to give the innocuous-looking fellow a friendly greeting. So he did neither, just
watched the man, and Trudy did the same.

"Good day to you," he said, nodding more vigorously. "Good day to you both."

"Good day," Trudy said in that unusual voice of
hers.

Upon hearing the sound of it, the man stepped
back a couple of paces and looked surprised and delighted. "Oh, my!" he said. "Your voice . . . I think
it really *is* you!"

"It's afternoon, my friend," Trudy replied. "Ain't
good for a man to get drunk this early."

"I'm not drunk," the man said. "Really. I've had
a couple of beers, maybe three, but I'm not drunk.
Just . . . intrigued. I have to ask—You *are* her . . .
aren't you?"

"Who?"

"Why, the Buckskin Belle! The woman gunfighter.
From the newspaper. You know, from Smithtown."

"The 'Buckskin Belle'? I don't know what you're talking about, friend."

"Surely you do! The Buckskin Belle . . . wearing buckskin clothes, like you are, and a pistol turned backwards. And you ride with an Indian, just like this one."

This was growing altogether too strange. And for Trudy, apparently, annoying. She made as if to stand up, and the thought crossed Kane's mind—and probably that of the pale little man, as well, because he grew even more pale and took another step back— that Trudy was about to pull out her pistol.

"Wait," Kane said, putting out a hand to keep her from rising. "Hold on. Sir, we don't know what you're talking about."

"Honest? Because if you don't know, you're the only ones who don't."

"What did you say about a newspaper?"

"Well, there's a big story all about the Buckskin Belle. Tells about her big fight over at Smithtown, how she gunned down a man or two right there in the town, then trailed some others out onto the plains and gunned them down, too."

Kane and Trudy shared a sharp glance. What had happened during the time they'd been traveling here, isolated and cut off from the world around? Had fame—or infamy—descended upon them without their knowing it?

"Where's one of them newspapers?" Trudy demanded. "I want to see this here thing you're talking about."

"I'll see if I can find you one, sir . . . ma'am, I

157

mean," the man said. He began looking about, on and under the tables, and at length gave out an "Aha!" and scurried over to a table on the far corner, where he retrieved a dropped newspaper. He unfolded it, scanned it, and nodded. In the meantime, Kane and Trudy noticed that every eye in the place was turned on them. It was not a pleasant feeling.

"Here you are," the man said, upon returning to them. He handed the newspaper to Trudy.

She took it, then just held it. "Forgot my specs," she mumbled.

"Let me read it, then," Kane said. She passed it to him.

Very conscious of all the eyes watching him, Kane scanned the article quickly. It was a reprinted article, actually, originally published in a newspaper out of Miles City.

Kane folded the paper and said to Trudy, "I think we ought to go somewhere and talk about this."

"Is it bad?"

"I don't know. Could be."

The man asked, "So are you her? Are you the Buckskin Belle? Because you have to be! Who else would be dressed that way, and have that voice, and be running around with an Indian? You are her, ain't you? Ain't you?"

Trudy and Kane ignored the man, left money on the table, and got out as quickly as they could.

In an abandoned stable tucked into a rough corner of the town, Kane and Trudy talked.

Kane read the story to her, every word of it, and

Trudy listened with rapt attention, at times appalled, and at times, Kane thought, maybe a little amused and even flattered that she suddenly had a public reputation as a gunslinger, with an appropriately dime-novel name to go along with it. Kane could understand how she could feel that way. Sudden fame thrust upon a nondescript life could affect anyone's ego.

But, all in all, Trudy was rather somber about it all, however flattering some aspects of the situation might be.

"That story's right in some regards, and way wrong in others," she said. "It makes that fight sound like something different than it was and me like somebody a lot different than I am."

Kane might have countered her on that. Trudy did have more than a touch of a Buckskin Belle quality about her.

"Is this going to cause us trouble, Kane?" she asked.

"I don't know. It's hard to say. There's always a danger when you get a public reputation as a fighter. Or so I've heard. Always somebody wanting to prove they're better. It was that way for me back in the Nations, though not as a fighter. I was a foot-racer, the best and fastest around. And I was constantly being challenged to prove it."

"Are you saying folks might start challenging me to gunfights?"

"It could happen. Or maybe that's just something out of the cheap novels the people back East like to read."

She paused. "Well, let them come, if they want. I reckon I can take them."

"Don't start playing games with this thing. It could cause you some true problems. It could endanger you."

She thought about it. "Or you, being with me."

"I suppose it could."

She pondered matters a while more. "Or maybe it will help you," she said. "Maybe your father will figure out that you're the Injun who rides with the 'Buckskin Belle.' And come find you."

"You never know." He paused. "It depends on how much he really wants to meet me. I'm not sure how badly he does. If he'd wanted, he could have met me in Colorado, but instead he chose to come here for some reason. He left me a sort of invitation to follow, but still . . . I really don't know why he handled it like he did. Or why he chose Helena as the place to come."

"What about this newspaper article? What are we going to do?"

Kane thought it over. "You may hate the suggestion, Trudy, but it may be time to get you out of the buckskins and into a dress again. It might save you a world of trouble."

She swore, shaking her head. "I'll not do it! I despise a dress! I'll not—"

"Trudy . . ." Kane was looking past her, toward the door of the stable, where a man had just appeared.

Trudy turned. The man was silhouetted against the light behind him, face and expression unseen. He wore a tall hat, tightly fitted denim trousers, and a loose shirt beneath a jacket buttoned at the top and hanging open at the bottom, the right side of it tucked back behind the butt of a pistol worn high on his hip. Its tie-down was loosened and dangling, the pistol available to be drawn at any moment.

"Howdy," the man said flatly.

"Afternoon," Trudy replied, turning to face him. "What can we do for you, friend? Is this here your stable? For if it is, we'll leave. We was just seeking a place for a quiet talk."

"Wasn't quiet enough. I heard a little of your 'quiet talk.' The Buckskin Belle herself! Ain't that something!"

"It's just a name some newspaperman has stuck me with."

"Are you as fast as they claim?"

Trudy glanced at Kane, who was thinking, *It's happening. The very thing we were just talking about . . . it's already happening!*

"Mister, we're not looking for trouble," Kane said.

Quick as a cracked whip, the man had a finger pointed at Kane. "You, Injun, keep your mouth shut! I'll take no talk from Injuns, Chinamen, nor darkies! I despise the lot of you! You're all no more than different shades of dung-on-legs to me!"

Kane swallowed down the surge of pure fury that ripped through him. At this moment he would gladly gun this man down himself, if he were a gunfighter.

The man turned back to Trudy. "I want to show you something, woman. Don't you draw on me, for I ain't going to shoot you. But I read in that newspaper story that you can draw so fast that your hand blurs out. You know what? That ain't nothing. You watch my draw."

The man stretched his right hand, wriggled his fingers, and suddenly the hand vanished and the pistol was gone from his holster, raising—

He had it no more than halfway up, though, before Trudy's pistol was out and cocked and aimed right at his head.

"You'll have to do a lot better than that, friend," she said in her most ominous voice. "Don't ever think you can draw on me without me drawing too. Don't even think about thinking it."

The man stood there, pistol half uplifted, his face now visible, clearly lined with stark terror.

"Put the pistol away, turn around, and walk out of here," she said. "Nobody ever needs to know about this. Just walk away. Walk away."

The man trembled, then lowered the pistol and holstered it. His lips moved, but no sound came out. He turned and walked away.

Kane looked at Trudy, who holstered her pistol and let out a long, slow breath.

"I think this Buckskin Belle business is going to cause a few problems," he said.

"Yes," she replied. "I believe it is."

Chapter 16

When Kane's pulsebeat had slowed to normal and the blood heated by the fire of confrontation had cooled, the sense of anticlimax that he had felt upon reaching Helena intensified into a mood as blue as the Punjab Star itself. A glance at Trudy O'Breen was enough to show that she felt the same.

It was she who first put in words the thought that had come to both their minds. "I don't know it would be smart for us to put up in a hotel or nothing tonight."

"I think you're right. Too many watching eyes in this town."

"I didn't look for nothing like this. Good Lord."

"I know."

They left Helena and found a camping site a mile or more out of town. There was still daylight left, which Kane regretted. He wished night could fall hours ahead of time. He wanted nothing more than to close his eyes and sleep. And to forget for a while quests, pursuit, danger. Even his hope of meeting his father.

So intense was this desire to forget everything that

Kane actually wondered if he was, down deep, simply wanting to lie down and die.

When the sun was going down and soup was cooking in a small kettle on the fire, Trudy sighed deeply and said, "I've put you in danger. I didn't mean to do that."

"Trudy, I've been in danger so much the past couple of months that I can hardly remember when I wasn't. It could just as easily have been Robert Blessed, the man who's chasing me, who confronted us instead of that gunman."

"What kind of man is this Blessed?"

"A wicked one. A persistent one. A man who'll stop at nothing until he gets his hands on that diamond."

She looked puzzled. "Diamond? I thought it was money he was after."

Kane realized he'd let slip something he'd kept from her, but it didn't really seem to matter. "I let you think that. I don't know why . . . maybe I didn't know you well enough at that point to tell you what it really was. It's not money. Just a diamond. The biggest, bluest, most valuable diamond there is. You ever heard of the Punjab Star?"

"No."

"That's what they call the diamond."

"What's 'Punjab' mean?"

"It's a place, far over the ocean, where the diamond came from. I've read some about it. It was mined in the Punjab region more than a century ago. It's been the possession of kings, princes, warriors, the church, and very rich men . . . until it disappeared a few years ago. It's been lost ever since."

"And you know where it is?"

"Not really. I have some letters memorized. When you put them all together, they supposedly will tell where it can be found."

"So why don't you find it?"

"Because there's one letter I've never seen. My father has it, or did. So there's no finding the Punjab Star unless I find my father and we put all the letters together."

"Is that why you want to find him?"

"No. I want to find him because I want to know him."

"But will you look for the diamond after you do find him?"

Kane thought about it. "I don't know. If he wants to. I admit, I've thought some about how it could be to have something so valuable. No more worrying about how to live, whether there's enough to eat. But I've been poor so many years nothing like that seems quite real. And as much trouble as the cursed diamond has caused me, a part of me hates it."

"I've never cared about money," Trudy said. "I know it sounds strange, but it's true."

"I believe you. I understand."

"If I was you, I'd say the devil with that diamond. When you find your father, you've found your treasure."

"That sounds like something a man I used to know and listen to, named Toko, would have told me."

"Toko. An Injun?"

"An old and very wise Cherokee who I've missed very much lately."

"Being rich can't make you happy. That's really true, even though folks claim that only poor, jealous folks say it. But you can have a lot of money and be miserable as a beggar, or you can be poor as a church mouse yet happy as a king."

"I don't think most people would agree with you."

"No, they wouldn't," she said. "Which makes me have to ask you something: Where did these letters come from, telling about the diamond?"

Kane realized with astonishment that this was a question he hadn't even asked himself before. He'd been so occupied with staying alive and memorizing the contents of the letters that he'd never thought about where they came from. And it was too late now; he'd destroyed the originals and their envelopes. All that remained of the letters was the memory of their contents in his mind.

"I don't know," he told her.

She was thinking deeply. "So somebody, somewhere, put together a bunch of letters that tell you how to find a lost treasure, and that somebody sent them out. Now, why would they do that?"

Kane was beginning to feel foolish. Though this question had come to mind before, he hadn't thought about it nearly as much as he should have. When a man was struggling to escape his foes and stay alive, he didn't dwell on secondary questions.

But why would such letters have been sent? Why indeed?

"It goes against all common sense and human nature that such a thing would have been done," she went on. "Most folks who care about such things as diamonds sure ain't going to go sending out letters telling somebody else how to get a big fat one that can make them rich. They'll go get it theirselves."

"Unless they had some other motivation than helping somebody else get the diamond," Kane said.

"Yes . . . or unless they was just plain loco crazy."

"Whoever did this wasn't crazy, I don't think. They were smart enough to put all those letters in a code."

"What kind of code?"

"Something similar to what stage magicians use when they're passing secrets to each other, doing tricks. This one I haven't managed to break . . . not that I've had time to work on it or have any kind of skill at all that would let me understand codes to begin with. But anyway, whoever sent out those letters couldn't have been crazy. They were very clever."

"Being clever don't necessarily mean you ain't crazy too."

He pondered that. "No, I suppose not."

Conversation dwindled away. By the time darkness fell, Kane was fast asleep.

The next morning Trudy said, "I been thinking, Kane. I come here to help you find your father. With what that newspaper printed about me, and folks like that little gunny after me, I ain't going to do nothing but hinder you. So I figure I'll be going my way."

Kane had anticipated this, and privately he concurred, but he had to make an obligatory protest.

"No need for that, Trudy. You're not hurting me."

"I'm hurting both of us. Folks have this Buckskin Belle notion about me now, and part of it has to do with me riding around with an Indian companion. As long as we keep doing things that way, we're asking for trouble."

"Maybe you're right."

Trudy seemed on the verge of emotion. "I'd have liked to stay with you and helped you find your pap, though. It would have been a bit like me finding my own."

"I wish you could stay." He meant it.

They cooked and ate breakfast, fed the horses. Trudy began preparations to depart.

"Where will you go?" Kane asked.

"Had a hankering to see California," she said. "Maybe I will."

"You have people there?"

"I have no people anywhere, nobody, now that my brother's killed."

"I'm sorry."

"You're the closest thing to family I got right now, Kane."

He didn't want to see her fall apart. He chuckled. "Why, Trudy, just the other day you were shooting at me, then chasing me down for stealing your horse."

"I mean it, Kane. I think high of you. I'm glad I run across you, and I wish I didn't have to leave you right now. Because I believe you're going to find your father in that town there." She nodded in the direction of Helena, which spat smoke from uncountable chimneys toward the mountain-country sky.

He could tell that such talk did not come easy for her. For a moment he wondered if he might have been wrong in his earlier perception that her interest in him had no romantic aspect.

"Maybe, when all this is over, we can meet up again," he said.

"Maybe."

"We'll have to figure some way to keep in contact with each other."

"Ain't no way to do it. I don't know where I'm going. You don't know where you're going or what will happen after you find your pap. We got no home, neither one of us."

"I suppose you're right."

She drew in a deep breath. "Well, Kane, I've been glad to know you."

"And so have I, Trudy. I'll be proud to tell people that I once rode with the Buckskin Belle."

They shook hands. There would be no embrace; neither she nor Kane would be comfortable with that kind of personal display.

"You take care," he said. "Don't let some hotheaded gunman looking for a reputation shoot you down." He paused. "Maybe you should find yourself a different set of clothes. Get rid of the buckskin for a while."

"Maybe. But what the devil. I ain't never tried to be nobody but me."

Kane gave her money, more than a hundred dollars, now making no attempt to hide how much he had. He trusted her now. She accepted the money gratefully and rode away before the moment became any more difficult.

Kane watched this unusual woman vanish into the Montana mountains, sure that he would never see her again. Certainly an odd human being, one who'd gone from fear-inspiring enemy to companion and true friend.

It was a shame indeed that some fool journalist's provocative scribblings had suddenly given a gun-fighter's name and reputation to a person who had wanted nothing more than to live her life quietly on her own terms and to help out a young half-breed who was trying to do the same.

He prayed that she would be well, and safe, wherever she went.

When Trudy O'Breen was gone, Kane broke camp, mounted, and rode back to Helena.

It was time to find Bill Porterfell. This time he wouldn't stop until the job was done.

Kane reentered town without drawing much attention. Now that he was not with Trudy he wasn't quite so noticeable. He rented a cheap room on the second floor of a firetrap boardinghouse, sat down on the edge of a dirty, worn-out, compacted mattress, and stared into a cracked mirror hanging over a wobbly table. On the table was a half-eaten piece of bread left by some previous occupant, quite crusted and moldy now. A broken comb, a crockery pitcher, a matching cracked basin, and a pair of rusted scissors made up the rest of the room's accoutrements.

He fell into a reflective, evaluative mood. The journey was taking its toll. He looked thin, weathered. His hair was growing long again, so he took up the scissors and gave himself a trim that altered his appearance to a degree that surprised him. Good. Maybe he wouldn't be quickly identified as the Indian companion of the Buckskin Belle now. Maybe he'd be left alone to look for his father.

Some new clothing would help, he decided. He'd obtained some fresh garb in Colorado, but since then he'd been through a train robbery that had injured him, recovered in a remote line camp with a murderous, restless cowboy, lived the entire adventure that had brought him and Trudy together, and then traveled through the cold Montana Territory winter all the way to Helena.

No wonder his clothes were hardly more than tatters and he looked five years older than he had only half a year before.

Kane walked through Helena's streets, trying to be inconspicuous. He visited a couple of shops and came out with his old garments fully replaced, with the exception of his coat. That coat he'd never get rid of, as long as its lining was the hiding place for his money. He was grateful for that money, a gift from a wealthy Texan, transplanted to Kansas, named Ben Flanagan. He couldn't have come this far without it.

As he walked the streets, he looked at the people

he saw—and some, to his displeasure, looked back at him, still recognizing the partner of the Buckskin Belle despite his change of grooming and clothing—and wondered about his father.

Might he encounter him around the next corner? Would he know him? Would there be some quiet, inner voice that would identify to him a man he'd never seen in his life?

Helena wasn't the biggest of towns, but it seemed quite huge to Kane just now. So many people, so many faces . . . he felt a rising anger at his father for having given him no means by which to find him. What good did it do to be steered to Helena if he had no way to pick Bill Porterfell out of the teeming human crowd once he got there?

He grew discouraged and headed back to his rented room. At once some warning instinct told him there was someone behind him, following, sneaking—

He wheeled around. No one was there. The boardwalk behind him was unoccupied, and there was no hiding place into which a follower might have ducked.

Kane felt tired and frightened. Now his instincts were failing him! He was beginning to feel pursued even when he wasn't.

He spent the entire day hiding away in his room, trying to come up with some sensible plan to find Bill Porterfell. But mostly he just paced about, going nowhere and coming up with nothing.

Chapter 17

Kane awoke the next morning in a different world. The bed had been uncomfortable, the room cold and drafty, and the room next door occupied by a man who must have been sick and in pain, considering how he moaned and shouted the whole night through. Yet when Kane finally slept, he slept soundly, and he awakened immensely refreshed.

He rose, washed out of the pitcher since the basin was leaky, combed his freshly cut hair, and dressed in his new clothing. He looked in the mirror and was pleased by what he saw and also by how he felt. No more indulging in dark thinking, as he had the day before.

Today, he vowed, he would find his father. And if he didn't . . . well, then, he would find him the next. Or the next. The point was to keep going.

The sun was out, the street brightly lit. It was still cold, a few flakes of snow spitting down from somewhere, though the sky was virtually cloudless. Kane strode along the same boardwalk upon which he'd imagined a follower the night before, laughing at himself for having done so.

At a café he ordered a good breakfast and picked up a newspaper bearing the previous day's date. The *Territorial Voice*, the banner read. Kane glanced over it and found it to contain typical frontier newspaper material—lists of public drunkenness arrests, accounts of brawls and the lawmen who broke them up, advertisements for liniments, land sales, cattle medicines, reprints of sermons, political speeches, and news from various outlying communities.

As Kane flipped a page, a headline caught his eye. His spirits immediately fell.

BUCKSKIN BELLE SEEN IN HELENA, the headline declared. Below it, a deck added further details: INDIAN COMPANION OF FEMALE GUNFIGHTER ALSO IN CITY.

Kane closed his eyes and shook his head. With a sigh, he opened his eyes again and read the story.

It was all secondhand, vague stuff, a compendium of various accounts given by people who had seen him and Trudy upon their arrival in the town. The inevitable rehashing of the shooting at Smithtown, told with even more lurid and entirely fictional details added, ended the account.

Kane folded the paper and put it away. Then, on second thought, he picked it up again, tore the story out, and put it in a pocket.

He was beginning to despise newspapers.

Kane paid for his meal and took to the streets. He still hadn't come up with a specific plan for how to find Bill Porterfell. So he did all he could think of, the same thing he'd done in other towns where he'd made this same search: He began buttonholing people he passed, asking them if they by chance knew any man named William Porterfell.

He found no one who acknowledged any such acquaintance but plenty of folks who eyed him with startled fear. Readers of the *Territorial Voice* or listeners to the local gossip, Kane figured.

The bright start of the morning was quickly giving way to a disappointing day. Even the sunshine was fading as clouds rolled in, the snow now growing a little heavier.

By the middle of the afternoon, Kane was ready for another meal. He headed back to the same café in which he'd eaten his breakfast. When he walked in, he noted a young man, very thin, intense in manner, with slightly bulging eyes beneath round spectacles. The fellow was talking to the heavyset proprietor of the place, a notepad in his hand.

As Kane sat down at the same table he'd occupied that morning, he saw the café proprietor gesturing subtly in his direction. The bespectacled fellow looked at him, his bulging eyes growing bigger.

Kane knew at once that he'd been the subject of the conversation between the thin man and the café operator. He sat there uncomfortably, unsure whether to ignore the young man's bug-eyed stare or to acknowledge it with a cold glance in return. He tensed when the young man moved, thinking he was coming his way, but instead the fellow sat down at a table across the café, one that allowed him an easy side view of Kane.

The café proprietor came over to Kane's table, act-

ing quite nonchalant but surveying him with study-
ing eyes. "What can I get for you, young fellow?"

"I'll have a steak. Biscuits. Water to drink."

"Water? That all?"

"That's all."

As Kane awaited his food, the thin fellow with the
glasses placed an order of his own, then sat there
looking at Kane while trying to act as if he wasn't.
Every now and then he would quickly scribble something on his notepad. Kane fought a compulsion to
rise and ask the fellow what his interest in him was.
Such an act would only make a scene, though, and
perhaps bring him trouble.

He reminded himself that the only thing that mat-
tered was finding his father, and he promised himself
he would focus on that, all the nosy, interfering
world beyond be hanged.

Kane ate his food in haughty disregard of the staring, scribbling stranger. By the time he was finished,
he'd actually almost forgotten the fellow.

But as Kane rose to leave, the other young man
did too and approached him. Kane faced him
squarely for the first time, and the other seemed to
wilt. If timidity were a smell, this fellow would have
reeked. But he was making a valiant attempt to overcome it.

"Sir . . . might I speak to you?" he asked Kane.

"Who are you?"

"My name is Kriger. Stanley Kriger . . . I'm a
newspaperman."

In Kane's eyes he appeared to be no kind of man

at all, just a boy, seeming younger by the moment. "Newspaper. What newspaper?"

"The *Territorial Voice*. Here in Helena."

"Let me take a guess. It was you who wrote the story about the Buckskin Belle and her Indian friend."

"Well . . . yes."

"Now I understand your interest in me. You're hoping to get a personal interview with the partner of the infamous woman gunfighter."

"I was . . . in fact, I was . . . well, yes."

"Why are you looking at me that way?"

"Because I didn't expect you . . . to sound so, uh, educated, you know."

"I'm an Indian, right? I'm supposed to grunt and talk like a savage. That's what you expected?"

The timid fellow was doing his best not to melt under Kane's intense glare. "I don't know that I expected anything in particular . . . I just didn't expect . . . what you sound like."

"It was my mother. She insisted I learn to speak English. I can even read. Quite well, in fact. I read your article just this morning. I can't say I was impressed."

"What do you mean?"

"What I mean is that you're spreading something that's false. There is no 'Buckskin Belle.' There's only a woman who happens to be skilled with a pistol. But she's not a gunfighter. And her 'Indian companion'—me—is no more than someone who is trying to conduct some very important personal business of his own that has nothing to do with your 'Buckskin Belle.' I'm not her companion . . . I merely rode with her for some miles—and found her to be good company. Not at all the kind to stick her nose into the business of others. She'll never make a good newspaper writer, I suppose."

Kriger ignored the cutting comment. "She was your . . . pardon me for asking this . . . your lover, then?"

Kane couldn't believe what he was hearing. Maybe this fellow wasn't so timid after all.

"I should knock you down for that." Anger rose, blossoming into sarcasm. "And maybe take your scalp. Do a war dance around your corpse with my face painted."

"I've made you angry. I'm sorry. I didn't intend to do that."

"Then what *did* you intend to do?"

"I intended to find out the truth about you and the Buckskin Belle. So I can write a story about it and do the job that I'm paid to do."

"You want to know the truth? I'll tell it to you. The 'Buckskin Belle' is a creation of someone like you. Some newspaper writer over in Miles City who apparently decided he liked the sound of the words and who didn't mind making up facts to replace whatever ones he didn't have. It's a trait you apparently share, if my reading of your story is any indication."

Kriger adjusted his glasses. "All right. Very well. I can see that you've been made angry. You say that what's been printed isn't accurate . . .well, then, sit down with me and tell me the truth. Tell me who the Buckskin Belle really is. And who you are. And what really happened at Smithtown."

Kane stared at the fellow, thinking. The other apparently misinterpreted this as silence born of rising anger, for he blanched a little and backed away.

"I will tell you," Kane said. "But not right away. I'll tell you after you do something for me."

"What?"

"I'm looking for someone in Helena. You can help me find him."

"How?"

"By writing something for me. Putting it in your newspaper. And if it works, then I'll talk to you. Tell you all about the Buckskin Belle, and about me. And the truth about the fight at Smithtown."

"You'll do that . . . and you'll not talk to any other newspaper?"

"I have no desire to talk to any newspaper, including yours. But I will, as a fair exchange, if you'll help me."

"So just what kind of help am I going to give you?"

"You're going to act as a go-between between me and my father," Kane said. "He's out there, somewhere, and you're going to help me find him."

Kriger took off his glasses and rubbed his eyes. When he put them back on he'd taken on a new, resolute manner. He put out his hand.

"You have a deal, Mister . . ."

"Porterfell. Kane Porterfell."

They shook hands.

"My office is two streets over," Kriger said. "We can go talk there."

"No. No office. Let's just take a walk around town. Bring your notepad."

An hour later, Kane walked alone through a steady snow back to his room, wondering if what he'd done had been a smart move.

Maybe not. Maybe he would regret it later. Or maybe it would be the very thing that finally brought his father to him.

He'd wanted a plan. Lengthy thought had not provided one. But a moment's inspiration, galvanized by the intrusion of an unwanted reporter, had done what lengthy thought could not.

He prayed it would work.

Kane entered the front door of the boardinghouse and mounted the stairs leading to his second-floor room. As he reached the top of the landing, he heard the front door open again, then close. Someone else was coming in. He thought nothing of it and went on to his room. He unlocked the door, entered, then closed and relocked it from the inside.

He lay back on the bed, thinking about what he'd just done. A direct and open approach to finding his father . . . an approach so simple it should work perfectly . . . yet because of its public nature, it could coil back on Kane like a snake and bite him. But a few risks had to be taken sometimes. Kane was growing accustomed to them.

Tomorrow, he thought. *Tomorrow's edition of the* Territorial Voice, *and we'll see what happens.*

As he relaxed and began to grow sleepy, he thought of Carolina Railey. The thought warmed him. She was waiting for him. Whatever happened concerning his father, she would be there. She'd promised him that before he left Colorado. He remembered her words, and the heat of their last kiss before he'd left.

Kane closed his eyes, missing her.

Suddenly he heard a noise at the door, a whisper, the scuff of a foot in the hall . . .

He sat up abruptly. A shadow moved outside, visible in the crack under the door. He was still wearing his coat, for the room was cold, and now he reached beneath it for the pistol he kept there.

He could still see the shadow in the hall. Someone lingered there . . . thinking of knocking? Of breaking in the door? Robert Blessed, perhaps? Some other curious journalist? Some reputation-hungry gunman hoping to locate the Buckskin Belle?

Or Bill Porterfell?

"Who's out there?" Kane called, loudly. "Speak up!"

The shadow vanished. Footfalls, heavy and fast, hammered back down the hallway.

Kane hurried to the door and threw it open. The hall was empty. Pistol still in hand, he dashed down the hall to the landing. He heard the front door open and quickly slam.

He ran to the window at the landing and looked out, but the porch roof below that window blocked his view of whoever had just left the boardinghouse.

Kane thought of running down and out, but realized it would be futile. There were too many alleys, too many places to hide.

Frustrated, Kane hid the pistol against his body and went back to his room.

Chapter 18

Stanley Kriger stood by the press, examining the first copy of the day's run of the *Territorial Voice*. Six pages this time—unusually big. Often the newspaper was merely one broadside sheet, front and back, and most commonly only four pages. Six was rare indeed, but welcome today, because it had made it easier for Kriger to slip into the paper, unnoticed, the item he and Kane Porterfell had agreed upon. Kriger's father, the editor-publisher, seldom looked closely at the newspaper, especially when it topped four pages. There was perhaps no reason to assume that the senior Kriger would have objected to the item's entry anyway, but Stanley Kriger had not wanted to take any chances.

If he could obtain the kind of interview Kane had promised him, reveal the full story of the mysterious Buckskin Belle, he'd make his name in the world of newspapers. He wanted this little scenario to work out perfectly, and with a lot of advance notice. He wanted to unveil his story about the Buckskin Belle with the aplomb of a sculptor opening the curtain on his latest creation. *That* would prove his journalistic worth to his always skeptical father!

Kriger made a cursory examination of the front page, then flipped through the paper. On page four, tucked away near the bottom of the fourth column, was the item. He adjusted his spectacles and read it.

He winced as he spotted one typographical error . . . but then, he'd done the job in a hurry. And the error was minor, nothing to make a difference.

He figured Kane would be satisfied. And if the item did the job it was intended to do, Kriger might just have a decent newspapering future after all.

An hour later the latest edition of the *Territorial Voice* was making its way around the streets of Helena, carried by the three newsboys who made a few pennies each week off the copies they sold.

At the front door of a boardinghouse far across town from the one that housed Kane, Robert Blessed, one of Helena's newest arrivals, stepped out onto the boardwalk for a cigar. A newsboy came around the corner, giving his call and waving the paper. Blessed dug out some change and bought one, then seated himself on the edge of the boardwalk, feet in the street, idly scanning the news while puffing his cigar.

He was halfway through the cigar when he froze, staring at the page. The cigar fell from his lips and rolled between his feet, where it lay ignored.

Blessed read and reread the brief article, which was really more of a notice than an article at all.

He couldn't believe his luck. He'd come to this town cursing how hard it would be to regain Kane's trail, or that of Bill Porterfell.

Now here it was, spelled out right in the newspaper and literally placed in his hand.

Blessed rose, smiling, and tore the article out. He folded it carefully and put it into a pocket.

That same little printed notice, meanwhile, had the attention of Kane Portefell himself. He sat in his boardinghouse, reading it. Kriger had done what he'd said he would.

Now he could only hope that Bill Porterfell really was in town and would read this same copy of the newspaper.

And respond.

Stanley Kriger sat at his desk, pen scratching on foolscap as he wrote out the last of several obituary notices that had come into the office from the local undertakers. Normally he hated obituaries, preferring to be out around town looking for stories, but today he was glad for a reason to remain here.

Every time the door opened, he looked up sharply, wondering if he was about to look into the face of Kane Porterfell's father. So far, that hadn't happened. Every visitor to the office had been from one or another of Helena's undertakers, bearing news of another passing to the world beyond.

Kriger dipped his pen and wrote out a final line. Blowing it dry, he looked over his work and felt proud. He was improving as a writer. Even his obituaries had a smoother flow.

"Son . . . a word with you."

Kriger looked up. His father was coming toward him, latest edition in hand.

"Yes?"

"What's this notice here? This Porterfell thing? Somebody seeking a missing father, something like that?"

"Yes. That's what it is."

"Then why are you interjecting yourself into the situation? This thing says that this"—the publisher scanned the item again to remind himself of the name—"this William Porterfell is to come see you, so you can arrange a meeting between him and his son, if I read this correctly."

"That's right. Porterfell's son thinks his father might be more likely to make contact through a third party—me—than to go directly to him."

"And why should you or this newspaper be involved in trying to bring this father and son together?"

"Because that's the price of the story I expect to get out of this in the end."

"What kind of story?"

"A good one. Trust me."

"Well . . . why is it run as a free news item? That sort of notice should be paid advertising."

"I know, Father. And usually I'd have handled it that way, but this time there is a good reason."

"We can't make a living giving away the space we should be selling."

"Father, if that little notice leads to the story I think it will, we'll be selling more newspapers than any edition yet."

"Do tell."

"You have to trust me on this one, Father."

"What is this big story supposed to earn us?"

"If you don't mind, Father, I'd rather not say right now. I'd rather reveal it to you when I have it in hand."

"In other words, just now you have bilge. And I've got an advertisement given away instead of sold."

"It's not an advertisement, Father. It's a notice that could lead us to a story that will make you proud. A story that I can guarantee will be picked up by every newspaper from here to San Francisco."

The senior Kriger gave a skeptical *harumph!* in reply—a sound that Stanley Kriger had heard time and again since he was in the cradle, a sound that communicated more clearly than words ever could his father's eternal doubts that his son would amount to anything better than a scribbler of obituaries and a setter of type.

Kriger was determined to show him this time. Even Eustace Henry Kriger, the seasoned, hardened, and forever skeptical publisher, would have to be impressed when his son revealed to the world the true story of the Buckskin Belle, told by her own Indian friend!

"You finished with those death notices?" the elder Kriger asked. "As soon as you are, I want you to go to the mayor's office. I understand there's some problem with the story you wrote about his plan for street improvements. He's hopping mad—and since you made the error, you can go fix the problem."

"What error? I reported precisely what he said!"

"Not according to the good mayor."

"And you believe him above me? I'm your son!"

"Just go straighten out the problem. And don't be giving away any more notices that should be paid advertising."

Stanley Kriger was obedient to his father's orders. He marched himself to the office of the Helena mayor, there to receive a chastising for a perceived error in a recent story. A minor matter, really, but the mayor was furious about it, and Stanley Kriger spent well over an hour practicing the social skill of graceful apology.

At length the mayor's ire was abated, and he grew more cordial. Stanley brought out his notepad and took endless notes on any and all subjects the mayor thought worthy of mention.

All the while Kriger was wondering if the notice he'd placed was stirring any attention.

When at last he was free of the mayor's clutches, Kriger hurried back to the newspaper office.

Toby Warren, the old man who kept the office swept and performed other functionary tasks around the place, greeted him outside the door.

"Man inside, waiting for you," he said.

Kriger's heart raced. Bill Porterfell, no doubt.

He walked in. There was indeed a man seated at the chair beside his desk, puffing a cigar and glancing at his pocket watch even as Kriger approached.

"Hello, sir," Kriger said, circling around to face the man, a broad fellow with a distinguished manner.

"My name's Stanley Kriger. I'm told you've been waiting for me."

"That's right," the man replied, smiling and standing, extending his hand. "I'm pleased to meet you, Mr. Kriger. I've come in response to the notice in today's edition."

"Would you happen to be Mr. William Porterfell?"

"No, I am not. But I am a friend of his, and he's sent me here."

"Who are you, then?"

"My name is Jackson," Robert Blessed said, smiling, the lie as smooth and palatable as creamy butter. "I've become a good friend of Bill Porterfell's in the last few weeks, and he's sent me to arrange a meeting between himself and his son."

Chapter 19

Kane looked intently at Stanley Kriger. "You're sure?"

They were seated in the same café where they'd first encountered one another. "Of course I'm sure. I talked to the man himself. Utterly convincing. I'm sure he knows your father."

"You think he's trustworthy?"

"Well, I suppose you can't know such things certainly, but yes, he struck me that way."

"Describe him for me."

"What does it matter? You've already said you don't know any Jackson."

"Describe him anyway. His name might not really be Jackson."

"He was tall, distinguished. Broadly built . . ." Kriger paused. "Kane, why do you have that expression?"

"He sounds like someone else I do know. A man named Robert Blessed."

"Who is Robert Blessed?"

"Somebody I hope never to meet again. Tell me, does Jackson have a beard?"

"No." This was true; Blessed had shaved off his beard before he went to meet Kriger. He'd also dyed his hair very dark, anticipating that Kane would ask Kriger just such questions as this.

"Gray in his hair?"

"No, none that I noticed."

"Did he walk with a limp?"

"I don't recall that he did." Again, this was true. Though Blessed had limped since the war, when necessary he could steel his will and concentration and walk perfectly, for a brief time. He'd done so at the offices of the *Territorial Voice*.

"It doesn't sound like it's Blessed, then." Kane suddenly felt weak. "I'm staggered. I'm stunned . . . I'm really going to meet my father, after all this time!"

"Yes, and then you're going to give me that interview you promised."

"Of course . . . *if* everything proves out to be as you tell me, and I really do find my father."

"What's the story behind you and your father? Why don't you know him?"

"It's a long tale, one I don't feel inclined to talk about just now."

"Maybe later?"

"Listen, I've promised you I'll tell you all I can about the Buckskin Belle. But I promised you no more than that. Don't become pushy."

"Very sorry. Pardon me. Well, then, let's talk about this meeting with your father. Where is it to be?"

Kane looked down at the envelope in his hand, still unopened. Kriger had brought it to him only minutes before. Kane flipped it over and examined the seal; it was unbroken.

"I'm surprised, Mr. Kriger. I would have assumed you would sneak a look at this letter before delivering it to me."

"I'm shocked!" Kriger said. "Do you think I have no sense of ethics at all?"

"My suspicion is that it's the seal, more than ethics, that kept you from opening this envelope."

Kriger lifted one brow a millimeter or so, saying nothing.

"Sorry," Kane said. "I've traveled a hard road lately, and I tend to be mistrustful of people."

"Well, are you going to open that letter?"

"Not here. In private. Sorry, Mr. Kriger, but my meeting with my father is something I want to carry out alone—and certainly not with full coverage from the local newspaper."

"So I'm to be left out, after all I've done to make this possible?"

"All you did was print a notice in the newspaper. And as I've already reminded you, our bargain said nothing about me telling you my life's story. Just about what I know of the so-called Buckskin Belle."

Kriger exhaled slowly and nodded. "Very well. But I do hope you'll tell me how your meeting with your father works out."

"I will. Not for publication, though."

"Of course not. But before I go, tell me where I can plan to meet you for our talk about the Buckskin Belle?"

"I'll be in contact. I'll come to your office . . . *if* everything goes as I want it to with my father."

"Good luck to you, Kane."

"Thank you. I could use it."

Night fell, bringing with it heavier snow. Stanley Kriger huddled in the darkness at the end of an alley across the street from Kane's boardinghouse. He watched the doorway, waiting for Kane to appear. He understood Kane's desire for privacy, but he'd be hanged if he was going to orchestrate a meeting like this and then stand aside. Besides, he had to be sure that Kane didn't try to run out on him and deprive him of the inside story of the Buckskin Belle.

He had an inkling of when the meeting would take place. Though he hadn't opened the envelope that "Jackson" had given him to take to Kane, he had examined it against a bright light and was able to make out the time of the meeting. But he hadn't been able to determine the place, or anything else in the letter. He had examined that seal a long time, looking for some way to break it without its showing, but hadn't been able to come up with anything.

So now he waited, and when Kane emerged from the boardinghouse, he would follow.

But it seemed Kane would never emerge. Stanley Kriger shivered in the dark alley for an eternity, blinking against snow that blew back hard against his face. What if Kane had already slipped out a different way? He might not be able to follow him at all.

At last Kriger was rewarded by the sight of the door opening and Kane emerging, looking to the right and left. Before Kane stepped off the boardwalk into the street, he patted his coat, and Kriger realized he was carrying a pistol.

This aroused a moment of question. What did he know of Kane, except that he had ridden with a known shootist and wouldn't say much about himself? What if his plan wasn't only to meet his father but to kill him? Kriger worried that his eagerness for a story might have led him unwittingly to a part in a murder plot.

Now that that possibility had come to mind, he truly did have to follow Kane. He watched Kane striding down the dark street toward an intersection and waited until he was rounding the corner. Then he emerged from the alley and fell in behind.

He'd have to be cautious; Kane would probably look behind every now and then to make sure no one was following him. Stanley kept his eyes peeled for recessed doorways, other alleys, parked wagons—anything that he might be able to duck into, or behind, if Kane should glance his way.

The snow grew even heavier and the wind was up. He pulled his coat high on his neck, scrunching up his shoulders within it, trying to maintain a pocket of insulating air between himself and the coat. He mentally cursed the bitter Montana Territory winters that every year made him dream of warmer, sunnier climes.

Kane was walking resolutely, but at one corner he paused and looked around, as if seeking a landmark. Sensing that Kane was likely to look behind him as well, Kriger slipped into a recessed doorway. Sure enough, Kane did look back, but Kriger had moved quickly enough. He was not seen.

Kane turned left. Kriger emerged from the doorway and went after him. The snow thickened, sometimes falling so densely that he actually almost lost sight of Kane for a few moments.

He hurried a little, not as worried now about Kane detecting him, because the same snow shield that muffled his view of Kane would muffle Kane's view of him.

By the time they'd covered another half-block, Kriger suspected he knew where Kane was headed. A cluster of old storage buildings, barns, and small warehouses stood in this area. It would be a good meeting place for people who didn't want an audience. Probably this was where Bill Porterfell's letter had instructed Kane to come.

Again, Kriger's instinct proved correct. He congratulated himself as he saw Kane pause in front of a particular warehouse, look at the name above the door and then at a sheet of paper—the letter, no doubt—that he pulled from his coat pocket. Kane shoved the letter back into his pocket and walked around the far side of the building, between it and another small warehouse.

Kriger crossed the street and went in after him. He was quite careful now; he had no way to know exactly where Kane had gone or where he would stop. Creeping through the darkness, squinting, trying to see, Kriger felt a combination of fear and excitement. This was why he was a journalist! This was what a journalist's life should be—not endless hours of boring typesetting, obituary writing, or playing to the whims of an easily offended mayor. Kriger felt a great sense of purpose, a conviction that what he was doing here was meaningful and important and *real* in a way that his previous journalistic efforts weren't.

He was still thinking such elevated thoughts when he rounded the next corner and something hard and crushingly heavy struck him on the back of the head, sending him face-down into the snow, there to lie motionless, stunned, surprised . . . and then to fade quickly away into cold senselessness.

Kriger was unconscious for a time, and though he could not say how long that time was, he sensed it was short. The cold snow on his face brought him to consciousness again. He lifted his head, looking into the empty lot behind the warehouse, a sort of un-planned courtyard in the midst of the cluster of buildings.

A battle was under way, two men desperately struggling. Kriger strained to see . . .

One of the two was Kane. The other, the man who had called himself Jackson. It was too dark for Kriger to make out whether weapons were in hand or whether this was purely a fistfight, but the impres-sion was strong that it was a struggle that might be mortal. These two fought like men obsessed.

Kriger didn't know what to do. He tried to rise but couldn't find the strength. He tried to shout but couldn't find his voice.

The fight went on, grunts and blows and terrible sounds. Kriger found himself weeping, not out of pain, because he was too numbed by the cold to hurt, but out of emotion borrowed from the combatants in the clearing.

Kriger began to fade out again, and this scared him. Someone had struck him, either Kane or the one he knew only as Jackson—more likely the latter. Yes, it had to be; Kane had been ahead of Kriger when he was struck. But why had Jackson hit him? Obviously because he didn't want Kriger to see what would happen in the clearing. What if Jackson proved victorious? He might come back, make sure that Kriger didn't come around again to name names and tell stories . . .

Kriger rubbed his face in the snow, trying to rouse himself. The fight, meanwhile, continued, motion in the darkness, the sounds of violence. Kriger managed to pull himself to his knees. He couldn't go any farther. Turning, he crawled like a child out of the alley toward the street.

He found an unlocked door to one of the warehouses. He managed to get it open and crawled inside. It was pitch-black in here and very cold, but not as cold as outside. He was beginning to feel sick, about to pass out again, but managed to get the door shut before he lost consciousness.

Kriger came around again maybe an hour later. He rose in the dark warehouse, pulling himself up along the wall. His head throbbed, but as he felt it he determined the skin had not been broken.

All was deathly quiet. He opened the door and walked out into the alley. The sounds of battle had ceased. He walked back, leaning against the wall, and looked into the lot. If anyone was lying out there, hurt or dead, the snow had made them invisible. And he lacked the strength to make a search.

Kriger returned to the newspaper office. He lived there, in a room above the office, serving as a nighttime presence in the building to keep an eye on the place. Cramped quarters but better than having to live with his widower father, in that unhappy house on the east side of town. He unlocked the front door of the office, staggered in, and locked it behind him.

He was exhausted and terrified. What had begun as an exciting journalistic foray had turned into a confusing, overwhelming nightmare.

Feeling too weary to climb the stairs to his room, Kriger went to his desk and sat down. He laid his head down to rest just a few moments, regain his strength. Then he would head down the street to his father's house, awaken him, and tell him what had happened.

Kriger glanced at the clock on the wall. It was two in the morning. He was stunned. He'd not had any idea it was so late.

He would not rest for more than a few minutes.

The clock ticked off one hour, then another. Stanley Kriger remained at his desk, unmoving, head resting on his arms.

Kriger awakened with the daylight. It took five minutes to make sense of why he was here—and why he had such a headache and the overwhelming feeling that something was wrong.

The memory came back in a rush. He glanced at the clock on the wall and the daylight spilling in through the windows, and realized how dreadfully wrong things had gone.

Kriger was tempted to panic, but he got a grip on his feelings. Whatever had happened in that clearing, it was now hours past. He didn't know the outcome. Perhaps the brawl had simply broken up and the two men had gone their separate ways. Maybe there was nothing to report to anyone, no reason to stir up any further trouble.

Besides, what kind of responsibility did he himself bear in this matter? What if Kane, or Jackson, was found dead in that clearing? Would Stanley Kriger bear any responsibility for having brought them together?

No reason to move too quickly or speak too soon, he decided. Not until he knew the lay of the land a little better.

Kriger went upstairs to his room, washed and combed himself into a presentable appearance, and changed his clothes. It was still early; no one would be arriving at the office for a couple of hours.

He would return to the clearing and see what he could find. See *who* he could find, maybe, though he hoped he'd find no one. He hoped he would never see Kane Porterfell or Jackson again. His much anticipated story about the Buckskin Belle didn't matter now.

He unlocked the front door of the newspaper office and exited onto the street. When he turned around after locking the door again, he was startled to find a man beside him.

"Who the hell—"

"Sorry if I startled you," the man said. He held up a rolled-up copy of the most recent edition of the *Territorial Voice*. "I've come because of something I read in here. I need to find a man named Stanley Kriger. My name is . . ."

"Don't tell me," Kriger said. "Your name is William Porterfell."

"Yes," the man answered, sounding very nervous. "It is. And I'm trying to find my son."

Chapter 20

Kriger could only stare stupidly for several moments.

"You're really Bill Porterfell?"

"Yes. Are you the person who put this notice in the paper?"

"That's me, yes, sir."

Bill Porterfell was a lean man, his muscles long and smooth and tapered, not knobby and hardened like those of a man who had labored hard at a single task for many years. From what little information Kane Porterfell had given to Kriger about his father, this seemed to fit. Bill Porterfell apparently was a man who had done many jobs and covered many miles in his time. His head was topped by thick hair, hardly grayed at all despite about half a century of existence, and he was handsome, with unusually intense eyes. There was a faint scar across his forehead, noticeable only when the light struck him from a certain angle. Another scar, much darker was always visible on his left jaw. His nose, thin and well shaped, appeared to have been broken sometime in the past, but the slight angle of the way it had healed had done nothing to harm the man's appealing looks.

Porterfell reached into a pocket, pulled out a scrap of newspaper, and waved it generally at Kriger as if the content of its words could thereby be wafted to him. "You say you can put me in contact with my son, Kane. You say that . . . young fellow, are you sick?"

Kriger had leaned weakly against the doorframe. "To tell you the truth, sir, I was knocked unconscious last night and spent the rest of the night passed out on my desk inside."

"Knocked out? Lands, son, how did that happen?"

Kriger looked keenly at Porterfell, examining his face, his eyes, his general manner. "You are him," he said. "You have the look of Kane about you. Oh, Lord, what a mistake I've made!"

"Where is he?"

"Sir, I'm sorry to tell you, but I don't know. I'm thinking that he's been taken prisoner by a man . . ."

Bill Porterfell tensed as though an electric jolt had passed through him. "A man? Not Blessed? Robert Blessed?"

During that walk Kane and Kriger had taken together, Kane had said quite a bit about the fearsome Blessed. "I'm afraid it probably is, sir," Kriger said. "I didn't know. I didn't have any reason not to believe him when he said he'd been sent by you. I should have been more careful. He said his name was Jackson."

"Oh no, oh, no," Bill Porterfell said, backing away, rubbing his chin vigorously, as if it suddenly itched very badly. "I don't even know anyone named Jackson, son. It had to have been Blessed." Porterfell began talking to himself. "I shouldn't have done it this way. I should have gone ahead and met Kane in Colorado. It's my fault, you know. They'd told me in Colorado that Kane had had trouble with Blessed. I shouldn't have gone away without making sure Kane was safe. Oh, Lord."

"It's my fault, Mr. Porterfell," Kriger said. "I'm the one who took Blessed to where Kane was. But he'd told me he was named Jackson. I had no reason not to believe him."

Porterfell paced intently back and forth at the edge of the street, just below the boardwalk. "Where did you take him?"

"I can take you there. There was a fight. I was knocked out myself, before it started. By Blessed, I'm sure. I'd followed Kane there, and I suppose Blessed saw me. But I did come to in time to see them fighting."

"Outside?"

"Yes . . ."

"In the snow?"

"Yes."

"Then there may be tracks. Mr. Kriger, I want to ask you to help me. Take me to where this fight happened. I might be able to track them."

Many miles away from Helena, a sleepy, rumpled man rose from a restless night and stepped out into the cold day. He shivered in the cold wind, but looked gratefully at the rising sun, anticipating its warming rays once it was a little higher above the horizon.

Spence looked around at the snowy landscape and felt sorry for himself. Here he was, cold and hungry and alone out on the prairie, his destination of Helena still far away. And though he'd finally gotten that opiate out of his system, and the gunshot wound that the Buckskin Belle had inflicted on him had begun to heal nicely and was proving to be even more minor than he'd thought it was, he was still a very tired and uncomfortable man.

He pulled some dry cornbread out of his coat pocket and began to nibble on it. It had crumbled badly and was now almost back to its original mealy state. But it took the edge off his hunger, which was all he asked of it.

Though he still had a lot of hard traveling to do, Spence realized he was actually quite fortunate. He'd been told he'd almost died of an overdose of that dope they had filled him with, but survive he had. And he'd managed to regain enough strength to attempt an escape, and darned if it hadn't worked! Now he was on his way to Helena again, to relocate that half-breed and find that Bill Porterfell fellow—and, in the end, put his hands on that missing diamond.

Spence finished his cornbread, went behind the shed to drain his bladder, then began walking. He'd not managed to steal a horse since his escape, but hoped he would be lucky enough to find one today. If not, he would head for the railroad tracks and hop a freight car. A freight car would be warm and safe. A man could sleep and travel at the same time.

Despite that bad turn of events that began in

Smithtown, Spence realized he was lucky. He was alive, free, and if all went well, he'd soon possess a share of the most valuable jewel in the world. Hell, maybe he'd possess all of it!

Spence strode on, heading toward the railroad tracks, listening for the noise of a distant train.

Kane groaned and looked up slowly into a face he'd come to despise.

Robert Blessed glared down at him, the lines around his eyes looking deep, his edges roughened, his entire look haggard. The pursuit of Kanati Porterfell had been hard on this man, and Kane could see it. Good.

"Well, you fought me hard, you redskin bastard, that I'll credit you for," Blessed said. There was a bruise forming above his left eye in evidence of the truth he'd just spoken. "But the fight and the chase are over now, boy. And I've won."

Kane thought about spitting at him. It was too much trouble, and he was so stunned and dizzy he'd probably miss anyway.

"Now, Kane, we're going to waste no further time," Blessed said, reaching under his coat to pluck a notepad and a fat pencil from an inside pocket. "You're going to re-create those letters, here and now. And there's no point in telling me you can't, for I watched you do it in Colorado. You can do it again."

"What if I refuse?"

"Then I kill your father. I've got him, you see. He's under close guard right now. I've hired myself some more help, and these men are the sort who'll kill as soon as I give the word."

Kane had no way to know if he was being lied to. "How do I know you really have my father?"

"You don't. So I suppose you're just going to have to take my word for it . . . or let me prove it to you by laying his corpse out before your eyes."

Kane looked around. He was inside some sort of big storage building or barn . . . No, wait—this was a stable. Ironically, the very same one in which he and Trudy O'Breen had paused for a talk, only to be interrupted and challenged by that eager gunslinger wanting to make a reputation by facing down the Buckskin Belle.

"How'd I get here?" he asked.

"How do you think, you stinking Indian? I dragged your sorry hide here. And I'll drag you no farther, nor chase you any longer. It should never have been this hard, you know. If you'd only cooperated, your father would have come to St. Louis, bearing his letter, and everything would have been so simple. We'd have translated the letters, decoded them, and followed their guidance all the way to the Punjab Star. And you would have been safe and sound . . ."

"You think I'm a fool, Blessed?" Kane said. "I'd have been dead, and my father too. You'd have killed us both once you had what you wanted. I had to take the letters to make sure you'd have a reason to make sure nothing happened to me."

"That time has ended, Kane. Tap into that remarkable memory of yours and write out those letters, every one of them. Do it now—or I'll send orders to have your father shot at once."

"Do that and I'll never write those letters out."

"But you will, because you have no choice."

Kane did spit at him then—and was pleased with his aim. Blessed jerked back with spittle dripping down his cheek. He cursed, lunged forward, and struck Kane on the side of the head.

Kane was jolted all the way to his toes, and his head throbbed painfully. The injury that he had suffered during the train robbery had gotten a little worse during his fight with Blessed, and this blow only increased the discomfort. He felt himself plunge momentarily toward unconsciousness, only to ascend again just as fast, hurting and almost sick . . .

. . . And changed. In that single blow, Blessed had pushed Kane past a vital point, snapped something inside him that had been strained and weakened over many a long and dangerous mile, many a fearful night, many a mortal ordeal.

Suddenly Kane didn't want to fight anymore. Didn't want to argue or scheme or seek strategies for survival.

He simply wanted to be through with all this, and if it cost him his life, so be it.

So he decided to do what Blessed said. "All right," he said. "I'll write out your letters. But please, when I do, let me go. Leave me in peace. And don't hurt my father."

Blessed was clearly surprised, having expected more resistance than this. He gaped for a moment, then chuckled. "I'll be damned! So you've finally gotten some sense about you! Good Indian! Good Indian! And I'll accept your bargain. You write the letters, and I'll let you go."

"And my father . . ."

"He'll be free to go. I don't need him any longer; he's already provided me the letter that he received." Blessed told the lie with practiced smoothness; he'd been lying to his own advantage for years. "Writing these letters now is your ticket to freedom from me. You give me what I want, and you'll never see Robert Blessed again."

Kane took up the pad and pencil. He touched lead to paper, then looked up at Blessed. "One question I have to ask: Why do you believe that this is all real? Why do you believe that you'll really find the Punjab Star?"

Blessed suddenly was intense, almost emotional. His eyes grew bright with a film of tears. "Because I *must* believe it! I have almost nothing left, Indian. Do you know what it is to be a man of wealth and power, only to see it all lost? When these letters began to appear, it was as if some force had arisen to spare me. Because I was about to lose it all, Kane. It was all disappearing . . . and then suddenly I had hope. The diamond! Something I was so close to possessing once, way back in Crosslin's Station in Kentucky, during the war. Something I never thought would appear again . . . but it will. And I'll be the man who gets it. And it will save me, Kane. It will be my redemption."

Kane stared at this man as if across a great, unbridgeable gulf, then shook his head, closed his eyes, and drew up from the back of his mind the contents of the first letter.

He began to write.

The snow where Kane and Blessed had struggled was plowed and tossed and dirty. Bill Porterfell examined it and imagined how fierce the fight must have been. He looked for blood and was grateful to see none.

"Mr. Porterfell, look!" Stanley Kriger said from the other side of the enclosed space. "You can see there where somebody's been dragged. See? There's the tracks of somebody, walking backward—you can tell that from the way the tracks look toward their fronts—and there's that double line where somebody's heels cut into the snow."

Porterfell came to Kriger's side and examined what the reporter had found. "You're a good tracker, Mr. Kriger."

"Who's dragging who, though?" Kriger asked.

"I have a suspicion that it's Blessed dragging my son," Porterfell replied. "If Kanati was lucky enough to knock Blessed cold, I doubt he'd have any desire to drag him off."

"Let's follow the tracks as far as we can," Kriger said, excited now, invigorated by the chase and oblivious to the earlier dizziness and weakness he'd felt.

Porterfell didn't reply. He was already following the trail through the snow.

*   *   *

Kane was rather surprised he'd been able to do it.

Given the abuse that his body, particularly his skull, had endured since he memorized the coded letters, he wouldn't have been surprised to find that the memory of them had been knocked out of his mind. But old Toko's memorization methods had done their job, and he found he was able to write out the letters, one by one, word for word, and hand them to Blessed. He considered deliberately changing them, rendering them useless, but if he did that Blessed ultimately would discover the ruse and come after him again, and all this would start over again just like before.

Kane no longer had the will to play games. Let Blessed have his letters. Let him have his blasted diamond.

Kane wondered even as he finished re-creating the final letter if Blessed truly had his father in his custody. But there was no way to know. He could do nothing now but hope for the best.

Blessed took the letters and held them in a trembling hand. He laughed and did a little dance there in the stable. "Oh, yes, yes! Hell, yes!" he chortled. "At last! Now only one left to find . . ."

"Wait!" Kane said, jumping to his feet. "What do you mean, one left? You said you had my father! You said he had already given you his letter!"

"Well, I lied," Blessed said, aiming his pistol at Kane. "I haven't yet found Mr. Bill Porterfell. But with you as my prisoner once again, that should be only a minor problem. He'll surely come running to save his son."

Kane roared in anger and lunged at Blessed, who danced back, cocking the pistol. "Ah, no! I wouldn't! I can as easily kill you as not. Your dear father would hardly know the difference, would he? And it would be a pleasure for me, believe me!"

"It's you who should die, Blessed. You're a scoundrel. A murderer. You're responsible for the death of my mother, and that alone makes you due to die."

"But what I'm going to have instead is riches. Nice irony, eh? It's the way of the world, Kane, and I . . ." He stopped. Kane's eyes had shifted, and he'd seen it.

Through a gap in the wall Kane had glimpsed someone moving, and it appeared to him to be Stanley Kriger. Just a flash, but he was almost sure of what he'd seen. Then another flash . . . another man, someone he couldn't identify.

"What are you looking at?" Blessed demanded.

"I'm looking at a liar and a murderer," Kane bluffed, averting his eyes from that telltale hole in the wall.

Blessed laughed coldly. "I ought to kill you right here. Hell, maybe I'll do it. Why not?" He cocked the pistol and aimed it at Kane's face.

Kane's heart missed a full beat. He stared into the muzzle of Blessed's pistol, unable to believe the man would *really* do it . . . then realizing, almost too late, that indeed he would. Kane ducked before the pistol fired, following some fortuitous instinct. The bullet sailed over his head and through the far wall.

"Help!" Kane called out. "Murder!" And he lunged at Blessed, knowing he'd have a better chance of disorienting and disarming the man by a direct attack than by running and providing a good target.

He hit Blessed hard, taking him down. The letters Kane had written out went in all directions. The men struggled, the pistol burning hot against Kane's skin but not firing again. Then, somehow, Kane lost his grip on Blessed's arm, and the pistol hit him across the side of the head, quite hard.

Kane went limp, now unable to fight. He would surely die, shot to death, right now . . .

But Blessed was more concerned about his letters. He let his last blow to Kane's head suffice and went about scrambling after the scattered papers. Meanwhile, Kane heard—or thought he heard—others entering the stable. He heard Blessed curse, then he was gone.

Kane lay there, eyes closed, unsure what had just happened but very glad to be alive.

Chapter 21

Kane opened his eyes when he heard noise, people approaching, and looked up woozily and warily. Stanley Kriger was drawing near, those buggy eyes magnified by his spectacles, shifting back and forth and all around, bright with excitement.

"Are you alone, Kane?" he asked, mindful of having been pounded from behind once already in the past twenty-four hours and not eager for the same to happen again.

"He's gone . . . I think," Kane said, his tongue thick. "He's got the letters now . . . lied to me . . . he said he had my father hostage already . . ."

"Not true," Kriger said. "Your father is with me."

Kane's eyes widened and he stared at Kriger. "Here?"

"Yes." Kriger waved to his left. Kane turned his head and looked up into the face of his father for the first time in his life.

Kane stared. It was all he could do. A moment he had sought for, dreamed of, had come at last . . . and all he could do was gape. At this moment there was little emotion beyond surprise, little thought beyond a superficial analysis of the man before him.

Bill Porterfell didn't present the most impressive image. He seemed overwhelmed to see his own son there, half reclining, half sitting on the dirty, straw-strewn stable floor, and looked as if he could consider fainting dead away at any moment. His face was pale beneath a veneer of tan.

Kane was disoriented and spoke more freely than he might otherwise have done. "You don't look like much," he said.

Surprising everyone, including himself, Bill Porterfell's chin quivered and a tear came. "You're the very image of your mother," he said.

Kane's own emotions began to stir to life. "She's dead now," Kane said. "She was murdered. But I suppose Carolina told you that back in Colorado, when she told you about me."

"Yes," Porterfell replied softly. "It broke my heart, Kanati. It's my fault, in a way. If I hadn't abandoned your mother so many years ago, I would have been there to protect her."

"If you hadn't abandoned her, there would have been no need to protect her. And remember, you abandoned me, too," Kane said. "You never cared about me at all." He frowned and blanched. "My head hurts . . . I think I'm going to be sick."

Kane leaned over to the side and vomited. "I'm sorry," he said, embarrassed.

Porterfell was struggling to control his tears. "I'm sorry, too," he said. "I'm sorry about everything. I know it doesn't change anything, but I am sorry."

"No," Kane replied. "It doesn't change anything. I only wish it could."

They took Kane to his rented room and put him on the bed. He wasn't badly hurt and was less disoriented with every minute that passed, but both Porterfell and Kriger insisted that he rest. He agreed, though with no intent to stay abed for long.

His father was here. As impossible as it was to believe, the thing he'd sought had happened. He had found Bill Porterfell.

So why wasn't he happy? Why did he look at the man and find that his predominant emotion was resentment?

Kane answered his own question by the query he put bluntly to the man who had sired him and then gone his way.

"Why did you abandon your own wife, Bill? She loved you all her life. She talked about you sometimes . . . and a few times I saw her cry for you, in secret. She was a good mother to me but lonely all her days. Why did you leave her?"

Porterfell was pacing back and forth in the room, smoking a small cigar. Stanley Kriger had been asked to leave, so father and son would have the chance to get accustomed to one another in private.

"I left her . . . because it was my way. I wasn't a good man, Kanati. I'm still not a good man. I've always sought my own way. I don't say it's right. It's just . . . me."

"Was she the only one?"

Porterfell blew a cloud of smoke. "You don't mind

being forthright, do you? Straight questions . . . but such deserve straight answers. No, she wasn't the only one. There were others. Three others, in fact."

"All Indians?"

"Yes. All Indians."

"You have a taste for them, I suppose," Kane said, making no attempt to mask the bitter tone creeping into his voice.

"I suppose I have. But none of the others was like your mother, Kanati. She was a special woman."

"A special woman you never came to see. A special woman who told me you were dead. A special woman who gave birth to your own child, and you never once cared enough to lay eyes on him . . . on me."

Porterfell slung the cigar onto the floor and crushed it out. "Is this why you came this far to find me? To preach to me about my evil ways?"

"No. I came this far because you chose not to stay in Three Mile, Colorado, where I could have met you long before now. But you moved on again—left me directions to follow you, sure—but you moved on. I had to follow, and I almost got myself killed along the way."

"I couldn't know that would happen. You can't hold me to fault for that."

"No. But you knew that Robert Blessed had pursued me. You even knew he'd had my mother killed. Carolina Railey told you all of that—she told me she did. But still you moved on, coming all the way here, and left me to fend for myself in finding you."

"I didn't know you despised me so."

Kane said, quite truthfully, "I didn't know it either. Not until now. You should have stayed in Colorado once you knew I was there. You shouldn't have run off again."

"If you feel this way, maybe I should just run off again."

Kane could tell he meant it, and it alarmed him. "No! No . . . don't do that." He was surprised by his own intensity, the rapid reversal of his emotions.

"I ain't never been one to stay where I'm not wanted," Porterfell said.

"Yes, but the sad thing is, you never stayed places where you were wanted, either."

"Well. Clever turn of phrase there. But I suppose I deserve it. And I suppose I do deserve your hatred."

Kane could easily have broken down under the emotional pressure of this conversation, but he held together. "I don't hate you. Not really. I'm just angry. I wish I could have known you when I was a boy. I wish I hadn't missed so much of what might have been. I wish I could have had a father."

Porterfell didn't seem to know what to say. He shifted the subject. "Remarkable, how well you speak. Your mother, I reckon, must have taught you."

"Yes. She told me I'd never make it in the white man's world unless I spoke as well as a white man. But so far, all the white man's world has given me is a run for my life."

"And for your father . . . and a diamond."

The diamond. Kane had almost forgotten it. "I

don't know whether I want the diamond. All I was looking for was to find you."

"The diamond would do you more good than me. I'm worthless. It's anything but."

"You're not worthless. I don't care about the diamond. I suppose Blessed will get it now, if it really exists, and if those letters really lead to it."

"But remember," Porterfell replied, "he still doesn't have the letter that came to me."

"That's right!" Kane suddenly realized. "He told me he'd caught you already and that you'd turned it over, but that was obviously a lie, because here you are."

"That's right. Here I am, and my letter, too."

"Where is it?"

"Up here," Porterfell said, tapping his head. "Memorized."

"Me, too," Kane said. "Except I memorized all of them. All but yours, of course. The only one I haven't seen."

"Amazing that you could do that."

"An old Cherokee man named Toko taught me how."

"I remember Toko."

"You do?"

"Surely. Knew him long before there was a Kanati in the world. Back when your mother and me were still together." Porterfell smiled, and something in that smile softened the edge of Kane's anger.

"I admired Toko," Kane said. "I suppose in a way he took your place."

"Umm. That hurts a little, Kanati. But if I'm to be

truthful with you, probably Toko was a better father figure to you than I ever would have been. I'm not a good man, Kanati. I'm unsuccessful, shiftless, at times dishonest. I've failed in every enterprise I ever undertook. But I hope you can find something in me worth thinking well of.''

"Tell me something. Did you want me to find you? Really?"

"Yes. God, boy, I ached to see you as soon as that pretty Cherokee girl in Three Mile told me about you and all that had happened to you, and how you were looking to find me . . . oh, how I wanted to meet you.''

"Then why didn't you? Why did you come here instead?"

Porterfell grew very serious. "Because in the most important ways, I'm not a brave man, Kanati. I've faced battle, dangers of all kinds . . . but a few things I run from. Settling down, for example. The married life. And things that have to do with the heart. I don't know how to deal with such things at all. So I decided to leave it up to you. If you followed me all the way to Helena, I would know you were serious about wanting to know me. If not . . . well, then, so be it.''

"How do you know it was you I came after?" Kane asked. "Maybe it's the diamond I want."

"I might think that if I hadn't talked to your Carolina. And if you hadn't told me just now you don't care about the diamond. Let me tell you, Kanati, the real jewel in your life is that young lady. She's beautiful, a rarer find than any diamond. And she loves you. I don't know if you know that."

"I know."

"Marry that girl, Kanati. Marry her and stay with her. Nail your shoes to the floor and don't wander. Don't be like me."

"I won't be. Whatever I am, I won't be like you. I'll not abandon my woman or my family if ever I'm privileged to have one."

Porterfell pulled out another cigar, bit the end off it, then just stared at it a moment before pocketing it again. He chuckled. "There's my problem, Kanati. I never quite know what I want."

"I do. I always did. All I ever wanted was a normal life, with a father and a mother. But I never had it."

"Because of me. I know. I make no excuses, Kanati. I should have done better by you." He looked at Kane. "You know, if I could put my hands on that diamond, I'd give it to you in a heartbeat. Just to make up for all the years, all the neglect. All I took from you."

"I told you—I don't want the diamond. I can't even really believe there is one. I read some legends, about Patrick's Raiders and Crosslin's Station and all that . . . but I can't persuade myself it's really true."

"Robert Blessed believes in it. He believes in it enough to kill for it."

"He told me it's his only hope of regaining all his lost wealth."

"If he found the Punjab Star, he'd have regained the wealth of a thousand men, not just himself. It's a jewel of amazing value."

"So the Crosslin's Station story is true? The Punjab Star really was there?"

"I never saw it. Not directly." Porterfell paused. "But I do believe it was there. And I believe I know who got it."

"I want to hear the story, Bill. I want to know what it was my mother died for."

Porterfell looked at his son. "And well you should. Well you should. And now is as good a time as any."

Chapter 22

Bill Porterfell gazed at the wall as he spoke.

"It's a strange story, Kanati. A story of a troubled time, of greed, of selfishness . . . and in the end, of tragedy."

"You're talking about Crosslin's Station."

"Yes. You've heard the story. The legend, I should say. Because it's become a legend. I've read some of the versions. None of them are completely right."

"Do you know the right version?"

"I was there. I saw what happened. I know the truth . . . as much of it as anyone knows, anyway. I know what I saw. And what my part in it was. I'm not proud of all of it."

"Tell me."

Porterfell drew in a long breath, paused, then began.

"It was in 1864. In May, I believe. The height of the fame of Patrick's Raiders. What a band we were! No one was more daring, no one was bolder. Especially the core of our band. A small band of the best and bravest of Patrick's Raiders . . . an elite little group who ran from nothing. I was part of that group, and proud of it."

"It was that core group who was at Crosslin's Station, right?" Kane asked.

"Yes. Just a dozen or so of us there, right in the heart of Kentucky. A dangerous place, Kentucky was in those days, being officially neutral but crawling with Yanks.

"Crosslin's Station wasn't too bad a place for us, though. Rebel sympathy was strong in that area, not a Yankee held dear for a hundred miles around. So we felt safe there, for the most part.

"But feeling safe didn't mean feeling satisfied. Especially some of us. Sergeant Robert Blessed and Corporal Jason Wyrick were stirring the pot, talking sedition against Colonel Patrick. They and Patrick had been splitting away from one another for months, but what it came down to that night was that they were angry because we couldn't rob the bank."

"Yes," Kane said. "I read something about that. Patrick's Raiders had been robbing banks all through Kentucky."

"So we had. It was a big part of our purpose. We'd strike small banks in little towns, just as daring as Missouri bandits, and take the gold and silver and federal notes and pass them on to the Confederate treasury. That's why some went to calling Colonel Patrick the Silver Raider, because of all the silver he brought in to the Confederate cause.

"But the bank in Crosslin's Station we were forbidden to rob. By the colonel himself. And this despite the fact that the bank was supposedly full of money at the time.''

"Why was that?'' Kane asked.

''The bank was owned by a man named Paul Hardison, who had a big house right there in the town. The colonel was an old friend of Hardison's, and a guest in his house that night, while the rest of us camped in a grove some distance away. And how the rumors were flying—thanks mostly to Blessed.''

Porterfell leaned closer to Kane, lowering his voice as if the rumors he was about to share were current ones, not dusty memories of a long-gone war.

''There was talk in that part of Kentucky at that time that an English fellow, very rich, name of Blane Church-Campbell, was at Hardison's house that night. Talk was that this English fellow being there was the very reason that the colonel had come to visit Hardison. This English fellow had something very valuable that he wanted to donate to the Confederate cause. Something he'd come all the way from England, to his friend Hardison, to give.''

''The Punjab Star,'' Kane said.

''That's right. The Punjab Star. At the time, you know, I'd never even heard of the thing. What would a man like me know of jewels, even famous ones? But Blessed knew all about it. He said this diamond was bigger than any other, and more valuable than a common man could even imagine. A diamond that kings would kill to own . . . maybe some already had. And he said that diamond, if it was there at all, was surely in the safest place that Hardison and his English friend could stash it.''

"The bank vault."

"That's right. And Blessed was talking about how it was a cussed shame that those of us there couldn't just take that diamond for our own. Sell it to some rich collector, maybe even some other nation somewhere over the ocean, and split the money between us. We'd taken all kinds of risks for the rebel cause, he said. It was time we did something for ourselves. And all this betraying talk he was doing right in the very hearing of Stephen."

"Who is that?"

"Who *was* that, you should ask. For he's dead and gone these many years, and that's part of the story of what happened that night. Stephen Patrick was the nephew of Colonel Patrick, but a nephew in name only. The colonel had raised him as a son, and loved him dear. Stephen rode with us, and he was a fine young soldier, brave and true, never flinching from anything. The only thing I could never figure out was why the colonel ever let Stephen ride with us at all, taking the risks we did. But he was proud of him, and Stephen was loyal to the colonel, true right down to the bone. He was always defending him before Blessed, who would downtalk the colonel every chance he got. Why the colonel let Blessed do like he did, why he didn't just rid himself of him, I'll never know. I wish he had. Things would have been different."

Kane asked, "Didn't Blessed worry, talking about robbing the bank against the colonel's orders, with the colonel's own nephew hearing it all? Didn't he fear that Stephen Patrick would report what he was saying?"

"I wondered the same thing at the time. It should have been a warning to me that Blessed already had it in mind to shut up Stephen Patrick forever . . . which he did before that night was through. But I'm getting ahead of my story."

Bill Porterfell rose and began pacing back and forth as he spoke. Kane waited for him to go on, though he was torn between wanting to hear the story and merely marveling over the novel fact that this man, this stranger, pacing before him was his *father*.

Porterfell coughed, then cleared his throat. "So there we were, us camped in that grove, the bank sitting there in that little town, the colonel up in this big house on the hill with the banker Hardison and a rich English eccentric who Blessed swore had parked the Punjab Star itself in the bank vault. And all the while Blessed talking about robbing that bank, defying the colonel. And then it all broke loose. Something nobody could have predicted. The bank got robbed. Not by us but by somebody else. It seemed there were others who had heard that this Church-Campbell was the supposed owner of the Punjab Star. Anyway, in the night this bell clangs, and there's a general alarm in the town about the bank being robbed. Five armed men, somebody said.

"Colonel Patrick, Hardison, and the Englishman all came out, Hardison and Church-Campbell all wrought up about what had happened and the colonel determined to do something about it. There was no proper police in that vicinity, so the colonel set us to the job of chasing down these ruffians. The colonel would have gone himself but for a muscle in his leg having been pulled bad a couple of days before, leaving him where he could hardly walk and was pained badly even to ride.

"We lit out after the robbers. There was a thousand thoughts going through my mind, and I knew what Blessed and Wyrick and maybe some others was thinking: Here's our chance to get what was in that bank without us even having had to do the robbing ourselves. We rode, pursuing hard, and in the end it come to a fight. Guns blasting in the dark, men crying out, guns blasting again, men sneaking about through the trees. We was well off from any occupied place when this happened, so the fight was seen by none but those who were in it.

"All but two of the robbers was killed outright. The other two begged for their lives, saying they'd give all the stolen money back to us if only we'd let them live. Nothing was said of any diamond at that point. Blessed tells them, Surely, we'll spare you just like you ask. So they turn over the money, in sacks, and as soon as he has it in hand, Blessed pulls out a pistol and shoots one of the pair through the head. Dead on the spot. He was about to shoot the second when I spoke up. I put myself between Blessed and this poor man and told him no. Don't you murder this one, I said. He's hardly more than a boy, I told him.

"Blessed, he looked at me in the moonlight like he

might shoot *me*. There's good reason to kill all of them, he said. If they're dead, we can take this money and hide it. We can tell the colonel it was hidden by the robbers before we engaged them and that we don't know where it is. Then, on the sneak, we can take the money with us, divide it out. Then he commenced to get ready to kill that last prisoner despite me.

"So I fought him. Struggled with him right there, hand to hand, Blessed with his pistol out. He fired in the midst of the fight . . . and the ball struck Stephen Patrick in the heart. The poor fellow fell dead right there.

"Blessed claimed it for an accident, but I didn't believe it was, nor do I believe it now. He'd planned to engineer that young man's death one way or another. But with Stephen down, that ended our brawling. We all gathered around, staring down at him, and none of us seemed to know what to do. Then Jason Wyrick spoke up. We can't have the colonel finding out that his nephew died at the hands of his own men. We all have to stick together, tell the same story. We'll blame the death on this one, he says— pointing at the one robber still surviving. And we'll shoot him dead so he can't tell the story any different.

"There was a general agreement to this . . . though I wasn't willing. But I knew it wouldn't do to say so. I had to make a pretense. So I stepped forward, told Wyrick he was right, and offered to take care of shooting the last robber myself. This notion appeared to amuse Wyrick, and pleased Blessed considerably. Wyrick handed me his own pistol to do the job.

"I won't do it here, I told them. Not before all these witnesses. I'll take him away in the woods, and do it there, and that way all can truthfully say they didn't see me kill the young man. Blessed argued against this, believing I was going to betray the cause and let the fellow go—after all, I had been fighting on his behalf—so I told Blessed that I'd let him come and see the corpse for himself when the job was through. This was agreed upon."

Porterfell paused a few moments, resting his voice. He continued to pace, and Kane found himself eager for his father to go on with his tale. He cleared his throat one more time, and then continued.

"I led this poor lad out into the woods, the moon beginning to hide itself behind clouds and then coming out again, hiding again, and so on. This poor boy was frightened out of his wits, weeping, believing he was sure to die. I took him well out of view of the others, into a sort of little clearing in the woods.

"He fell on his knees there and begged me not to shoot him. He was talking fast as a running horse, and what he told me surprised me. He said he was named Nathan Hardison, that he was the very son of Paul Hardison, the owner of the robbed bank. He told me he had been the mind behind the robbery and had gathered up the robber band and planned the entire thing. His motive, he said, was vengeance. He and his father had fought terribly, taking different sides on the war, different views on religion, on questions of right and wrong, on every kind of thing, to the point that the banker had written him right out of his will in spite. The son, more spiteful yet, decided to even the score with his pap by emptying his bank of money. The young fellow begged me to spare him and told me that if I would, he would give me something worth more than all that stolen money . . . something he said was the real treasure in that bank."

Kane nodded. "The diamond."

"So he said. And having heard Blessed talking it up so much, I admit I listened. I asked him why the diamond wasn't with the money, which was already in the hands of Blessed and the others, and he said it was because he'd hidden it after the bank robbery. If I'd spare him, he said, I could have the diamond. He'd tell me where to find it.

"The truth was, Kanati, that I'd planned to spare him anyway if he had the brass about him to pull off the trick I had in mind, but by now I was curious about that diamond. I told him I'd spare him if he'd tell me of it. He said the diamond was in a small box, and he'd stashed it in a hole in a sycamore tree at the edge of the woods while he and the other robbers were making their dash. He described the tree. The others hadn't known about the diamond, he said; it had been his plan to keep that for himself.

"I thanked him for telling me, and he rose as if to leave. No, I said, you can't go. We have to make them think you're dead. I told him that I was going to shoot him through the shoulder, so they'd hear the shot, and that he'd have to spread blood on himself and lie there still as death when another man came up to make sure he *was* dead. This fellow didn't favor this notion, of course, but I knew it had to be. I told him I'd try to shoot him so the bleeding wouldn't be too bad, and before he could protest more I plugged one through his left shoulder.

"He passed out from the shock and the pain, which was well and good in that I didn't think he'd have it in him to pretend to be senseless if he was hurting. I spread some of the blood that was coming up out of the wound down around the area of his heart, to make it appear I'd shot him there, then looked up and was pleased to see the moon scooting behind a big bank of clouds. The darker the better, for what had to be done now.

"I went back to Blessed, who of course had heard the shot, and told him that the job was done. Meanwhile, I was dismayed to see every man among our band poking around in the trees, looking in stumps and under logs and so on, no doubt having looked for the diamond among the money, not found it, and decided that maybe it had been hidden. Blessed, meanwhile, came back and took a look at the fellow I'd shot. Young Hardison was passed out there, and it was dark enough with the moon behind the cloud that you couldn't see him breathing shallow, like he was. Blessed was satisfied that he was in fact dead, and he kicked a few leaves and branches across him and left him where he was.

"When we got back to where the search was going on, the moon came out again, and what did I see but Mack Brennan, one of the Raiders, with his arm stuck in a hole in a sycamore at the edge of the woods—

by description the very tree where the diamond was hid. I walked up to him. Anything there? I asked. No, he says. Nothing. But as I walked away, I sure thought I saw him stuffing something under his coat.

"The search ended after a time, for we had to get back before it all started looking questionable. We took the stolen money, hiding it in our clothes, our saddlebags, and so on. Thank God they didn't try to carry the dead back, for that would have exposed that the Hardison boy was still alive. Of course, I was the only one of the Raiders who knew that he was the banker's own son.

"We did, of course, take back the body of Stephen Patrick, and to spare the colonel more pain, we told him he had been killed by one of the robbers. I wished after that I'd told him the truth, for something could have been done with Blessed, and what happened to the colonel a little later wouldn't have happened at all.

"The colonel was devastated, ruined, by the death of Stephen. We told Hardison that the money had been hid by the robbers and that we didn't find it, and that he'd need to search the woods by daylight to see what they'd done with it. But he didn't seem as worried about the money as he—and the Englishman—were about something else they wouldn't name. I can only suppose it was the Punjab Star—which I believed then, and believe to this day, had been found in that hollow tree by Brennan.

"We left Kentucky for Tennessee, bearing the body of Stephen Patrick with us. The colonel hardly spoke a word. The fire was gone from him. Then, on the way back, he was shot by snipers. Or so the story went. Blessed and Wyrick were noticeably absent at that moment, and I believe they did it. Because there were Yanks about at the time, we were never able to recover the colonel's body.

"A day later, Brennan was gone. Just vanished. Left with his diamond, I suppose, and I never heard from or of him again. I've always wondered if he changed his name, took off to Europe, maybe, and lived like a king. Who can say?

"Anyway, with Colonel Patrick dead, there was no more Patrick's Raiders. We just all dissolved away, and at last the war ended and that was that. Every one of us had a bit of the money taken from that bank—as I admitted to you, Kanati, I'm not proud of everything I did at that time—but few of us, that I know of, had success with it. Mine was gone very soon. Typical of me to lose money.

"Robert Blessed and Jason Wyrick had managed to get more of the money for themselves than anyone else had, and they partnered up and went into a hundred different dishonest schemes and businesses, as I hear it told. Did well for themselves."

Kane said, "They're not doing well now. Blessed told me himself that he was almost out of money. That's why he is so determined to get the Punjab Star."

"If he does get it, I hope he chokes on it. Or I hope it drives him mad, like the legend says."

"What legend?"

"You haven't heard that? The diamond is cursed.

So goes the story, anyway. Whoever owns it, they say, becomes possessed by it. Goes mad."

Kanati was thoughtful. "There's something I don't understand. If this Brennan fellow had the diamond, he would have had to sell it to benefit from its value. But if he had sold it, the diamond would be accounted for today. It wouldn't still be considered lost."

"I've thought of that myself, Kanati. I don't know the answer to that one. But I'm told there are people who collect things, and that sometimes this kind of folk can be happy just having something, knowing it's theirs, even if they never do a thing with it or make a cent off it. It could be a situation like that. It's a great unanswered question to me."

"And there's another question, too," Kane said. "It's a question I didn't have time to ask myself very deeply until lately. It's just . . . why? Why would anyone who had a diamond that valuable send out coded letters to a bunch of old soldiers scattered over states and territories, telling them where to find the diamond? If someone had the diamond, wouldn't they want to keep it for themselves? Why would the possessor of the Punjab Star send out such letters?"

Bill Porterfell looked at his son. "I've pondered the same question myself, Kane. And I've reached only one possible answer: They wouldn't."

"Then who did?"

"I don't know the answer . . . but I think I might know where to find it. I didn't come all the way here for no reason, you should know. I didn't just pick Helena off a map and decide to come here."

"What are you talking about?"

Bill Porterfell didn't answer. His attention had turned suddenly to the door.

Kane heard it, too, just then.

Someone was out there, on the other side.

Chapter 23

Kane whispered urgently, "This happened before. Someone out in the hall. I tried to discover who it was, but he fled. I thought at the time it might be you."

"Wasn't me," Bill Porterfell whispered, then laid a finger to his lips and stepped lightly across the room. He put his hand on the latch, yanked it open . . .

Stanley Kriger spilled into the room. He'd been crouching out there, ear to door panel. Scrambling to his feet with as much dignity as he could muster, he looked, red-faced, from Porterfell to Kane, then found fascinating things to stare at between the toes of his shoes.

"So now you know," Bill Porterfell said. "You've got the entire story."

Kriger, with an exertion of will, looked up, swallowed his embarrassment, and said, "Not all of it." He stared frankly at Porterfell. "Sir, are you really chasing the Punjab Star?"

"I don't know why I should speak about any of this before a young scoundrel who listens to private conversations through doors, no doubt with the intent of publishing it all."

"Sir, I wouldn't do that. You must believe me. I was simply overwhelmed with curiosity. Now I'm even more so."

"I should run you out of here . . . but you did help me find my son. Besides, you know Helena better than I do. You might prove helpful."

"Go ahead and speak before him, as far as I'm concerned," Kane said. "I'm tired of hiding and lying and concealing."

"Very well . . . but you write none of this without my approval," Porterfell said to Kriger.

Kriger gave a pained look, then nodded. "Fine."

"The truth is, I'm not after the Punjab Star," Porterfell said. "I don't believe the Punjab Star is going to be found. But I believe someone here wants the members of Patrick's Raiders who were at Crosslin's Station in 1864 to believe it can be."

"But who would do such a thing?" Kriger asked.

Porterfell didn't answer at once. Instead he walked over to a window on the west side of the room, pulled back the ragged curtain, and squinted against the white light of the snowy world outside. He searched the distance, then spotted what he was looking for.

"I think the answer to your question, Mr. Kriger, lives in that house up there on the mountainside."

Kriger went to the window and looked out. He said, "The Proctor house?"

"The Patrick house would be a more accurate name for it."

Kriger gaped at him. "You mean . . ."

Porterfell nodded.

"Patrick?" Kane repeated. "Is that what you said?"

"Yes," Porterfell replied, still staring at the dark spot on the snow that marked the big house on the mountainside.

"But not Colonel Patrick. It couldn't be. He's dead."

"Is he?" Porterfell asked. "We never found his corpse after he was shot. And I ran into an old friend about three years ago. Jimmy Medford, former member of Patrick's Raiders and participant in the Crosslin's Station incident. He told me a story, a rumor that I didn't quite believe could be true at the time. He said that Colonel Patrick was still alive and living in a house on a mountainside beyond Helena. I laughed at the notion. Now I'm not laughing. I'm thinking hard instead, and the more I think, the more sure I am that the answer to the riddle of those coded letters and the Punjab Star and all this nonsense lies up on that mountain there."

Kane rose from the bed and joined the others at the window. "So that's why you came to Helena."

"That's right. I wanted to find out the truth about all those rumors."

"And did you?"

"Not yet. Mr. Kriger, do you know anything of the so-called Proctor house or the people in it?"

"Only that they're seldom seen and reportedly very wealthy—and not prone to welcome visitors."

"Well," said Bill Porterfell. "They're going to receive one, very soon."

"Not just one," Kane added. "I'm going with you.

I've been through too much hell not to get to the root of this."

"I think I'll go along too," Kriger said.

Porterfell looked at him. "No. You won't."

Kriger opened his mouth to argue, but the expression on Bill Porterfell's face cut him short. He smiled wanly. "No, I suppose I won't," he said. "Though if you find out that the Proctors are really the Patricks, and that the most famous lost diamond in the world is here, you're not going to keep me from publishing it."

"What if I threaten to shoot you if you do?" Porterfell asked. It wasn't easy to tell how serious he was.

"I'll just have to take the chance," Kriger said. "That's a story that just might be worth some risk."

Bill Porterfell opened his mouth to say more, then clamped it shut again. For the moment, there would be no more argument.

For the second time that day, Kane pulled the letters from his memory and put them on paper. Bill Porterfell, meanwhile, did the same with the single letter he'd memorized, and when they both were done, they placed all of them together in a stack and stared at it for a few moments.

"There it is," Porterfell said. "If we're to believe such a thing, there's the way to the Punjab Star."

"They're coded. Can you break the code?" Kane asked.

"I can. Indeed, anyone who was part of the core of Patrick's Raiders can. It's nothing but an old code we used to use to communicate with each other in the field. I saw that right away from the letter that I received."

"Do you remember what the postmark was on that letter?"

"Denver. But no name, nothing to give any further clues. Just like these others."

"Bill," Kane said, "do you want to find the diamond?"

"If it still remains to be found, I'd not mind being a wealthy man. But we won't find that diamond, Kanati. I feel sure of it."

"You have a suspicion of what all this is really about."

"Yes."

"Tell me, please."

"Later. I'd like to see first how close my notion is."

Kane was instantly suspicious. Bill Porterfell was going to decode the letters, play evasive, downtalk the possibility of the diamond's really being available for finding, and then snatch it for himself and be gone, just like before.

Kane had told himself he didn't care about the diamond, but this suspicion evoked unexpectedly strong anger. He would keep an eye on Bill Porterfell!

"Are you going to decode them now?"

Porterfell nodded. "No time better than the present, I suppose." He scratched his stomach and rubbed the back of his neck with his other hand. "I sure could use a drink just now."

"You drink a lot?"

"Too much, I suppose. It's another thing I'm not proud of."

"I have nothing to offer you."

Porterfell shrugged. "It's for the best."

Kane watched as Porterfell sat down at the little table in the room and examined the first of the eight letters. On a scrap of paper he began to write, slowly and laboriously, then looked at the letter again, scratching out a few of the marks he'd made and replacing them with others. "Not used to doing this," he explained. "It's been a lot of years since I used this code."

Kane lay back on the bed, closing his eyes. Stanley Kriger paced the room, restless, excited, finally beginning to piece together in his mind a full understanding of what was going on here. The young journalist saw the biggest story he could have dreamed of, falling together all around him, the kind of story that would get the attention of the big Eastern newspapers and provide him a chance at last to escape the oppressive grip of his eternally unpleasant father.

Kriger went to a window and looked out. "Great day!" he exclaimed. "It's clouded over and snowing." He peered at the sky. "Heavy clouds . . . we may be in for a blizzard."

Porterfell kept on decoding, chewing now on an unlighted cigar, growing ever more absorbed in his work.

Kane had dozed off when Porterfell came to his feet, paper in hand. Kane opened his eyes. His father was frowning.

"I don't understand," he said. "I've decoded it

correctly . . . I know I have, but it doesn't make sense."

"What do you have?" Kriger asked.

"Several sentences . . . but it's all talk about nothing."

"Does it mention the Punjab Star?"

"Yes, but nothing to tell me where it might be. Beyond the bare mention of the diamond, there's nothing but . . . Wait a minute . . . wait a minute! This thing might be double-coded."

"What does that mean?" Kane asked.

"It was something we did from time to time when a message was particularly important. We would in effect perform our code twice, so that the message obtained through the first decoding was itself a collection of further codes. You had to go through the process twice to get the final result."

"By all means, try it!" Kriger urged.

Porterfell sat down and studied the message closely. "If I've made any errors thus far, it could throw off the final message," he said. "Say a prayer, gents, that I can get this right."

Kriger stood over Porterfell's shoulder, watching him work, until a sharp glance from Porterfell sent him a message of his own that he heeded quickly, moving away and back to the window, where he looked out again.

"Snow's falling harder now," he said. "Look how dark it's getting out there, and it's still daytime."

Five minutes later, Porterfell stood up. "I've got it!" he declared.

"What does it say?" Kane asked.

"It says the Punjab Star can be found on the mountain that shines."

"And where is this mountain?"

"Just where I'd come to suspect it might be. Right here . . . or nearby. In the mountain ranges beyond Helena." Porterfell slapped the paper. "That's where it's to be found, boys, if it's to be found at all. And if what I've heard rumored is true, I think I know who sent these letters, and maybe even why."

"Who? Who?" asked Kriger.

Porterfell put the paper in his pocket. "Colonel Patrick himself, gents. Colonel Patrick himself."

Chapter 24

"But it's impossible," Kane said, rising and standing. "Do you really believe the colonel is still living? Just on the basis of some rumor you've heard?"

"On the basis of a rumor alone, no. On the basis of a rumor combined with these letters, letters that were written by someone knowledgeable of the communications code of Patrick's Raiders, someone who might have motives of his own for performing such a strange stunt as this one . . . on that basis, I can believe it's at least possible. The key to this mystery is the motive. Always has been. What possible reason could anyone have for doing such a strange thing as sending out coded letters, supposedly giving directions to a hidden jewel that any sane person would want to keep for himself? And if you can figure out a motive, then the next question is, Who would have such a motive? Pondering on that is what brought me to Helena. And if Blessed had kept his head about this instead of getting all caught up in a blind lust for wealth, he'd have asked himself the same questions."

"So what happens now?" Kane asked.

"What happens, I suppose, is that we go pay a call at the so-called Proctor house and see if that rumor might be more than just a rumor."

"When will we go?" Kane asked.

"As quickly as you feel able. How's your noggin?"

"Fine . . . or if not, I've grown used to the headache. I say we go now. I'm ready for this to end. I'm ready to know the truth."

Kriger stepped up. "And what about me? Will you make me miss such a story?"

Porterfell replied, "Young man, I'm afraid this quest is a bit too much on the personal side for it to be undertaken with the newspaper lurking in the shadow, ready to print it all."

Kriger looked angry, a red surge darkening his slender face, his bugged eyes narrowing. But Bill Porterfell had a quietly overwhelming manner about him, and Kriger shrank away and began to look sad.

"I'm truly sorry, Mr. Kriger," Kane said.

"So am I." He paused, then said, "Maybe, when this is done, we can reconsider?"

"Maybe. We'll see. By the way, Mr. Kriger, thank you for your interest, and your help."

" 'Thank you,' he says," Kriger muttered. "As if I can publish a 'thank you.' " He slapped on his hat, closed his coat, and headed for the door. He left without a further word.

At the window a few moments later, Kane and Bill Porterfell watched Kriger striding away across the street below. The snow was falling fast and piling up thickly.

"It's for the best," Porterfell said. "I rather like that

young man, though I certainly haven't had time to say I truly know him. But Lord knows, we don't need a journalist following us about. I don't know what we're going to find."

Kane said, "I didn't know what you'd think of me going with you. To tell the truth, I'd wondered if you might have it in mind to take all the letters and go off for the diamond yourself."

"No such plan, no such plan. Besides, I still don't really believe we're going to find that diamond at all. I don't believe the diamond is what this is all about."

"What, then?"

"Maybe revenge."

"For what?"

Porterfell smiled mysteriously. "I tell you what, Kanati. Let's just see what we find, and leave the speculation alone for now. Including my own."

"Fair enough. Are we ready to leave?"

"I don't see why not. But let's keep a sharp eye. Blessed may be out there, watching for us."

If Blessed was there, they didn't see him. They walked through the mounting snowstorm along the streets of Helena, through town and then out of it, along the lonely road toward the stony mountain where the Proctor house stood, even now vaguely visible to them whenever the snow let up for a few moments.

They walked with few words, private men shielded by the veil of fast-falling snow, glad for it despite the discomfort and cold, because they did not want to be seen.

Their course took them along a winding route that soon began to climb. Kane panted for breath, still weak from his ordeals, and Porterfell said, "Perhaps we're pushing you too hard. Perhaps we should go back."

"No," Kane said. "We must go on. We're too near the end of this to stop now."

"We don't know it's the end."

"It is. I can feel it."

Porterfell said, "To tell you the truth, so can I."

Another half hour of travel took them to the base of the mountain on which the Proctor house stood. It was invisible to them from this point because of the terrain, but the road was steep, and the house no more than a mile from where they were.

They climbed, their breath coming in labored gasps now. They made no conversation.

Halfway up, Porterfell seized Kane's arm. "Something coming up behind," he said. "Quick . . . off the road."

Kane didn't ask why they were hiding, but he was glad to do it. Instinct right now screamed for caution and stealth. They dropped behind a fallen, snow-covered tree beside the road, getting out of sight just in time to avoid being seen by the driver of a wagon that came laboring up through the snow, drawn by two steaming horses. The snow muffled much of the wagon's noise, and Kane was glad for his father's keen ears. Otherwise he might not have heard the wagon in time to avoid being seen.

Kane eyed the driver, who rode past them utterly

unaware of their presence. He heard his father whisper an almost inaudible expression of awe.

"It's *him*!" Porterfell said when the wagon was well past them. "I'd swear on anything you wanted that the driver was Colonel John Lindsey Patrick himself!"

"It can't be," Kane said. "That man was far younger than Colonel Patrick would be."

"I know that," Porterfell said a little brusquely. "I'm not a fool. But the image of him . . . it was the same. I swear. Like a much younger twin, if such a thing could be."

They left their hiding place and returned to the road, walking in the ruts left by the wagon.

The snow was falling harder than ever, the day as dark as sunset, when they reached the edge of the yard of the Proctor house. There they stood, looking at the house.

"What now?" Kane asked.

"I'm not sure," Porterfell admitted. "I suppose we'll just have to go up and knock on the door."

"I feel reluctant," Kane said.

"So do I, for some reason," Porterfell said. "But we can't very well go back in this weather. We'd freeze before we made it all the way into town."

Kane's shaking body and the icy grip the cold had on the core of him vouched for the truth of Porterfell's last statement. "Then we may as well screw up our courage and move on," he said.

"That's the spirit. Say a prayer, boy. I don't know what we'll find here."

They proceeded on through the yard, toward the porch, when the door of a woodshed they'd just passed opened, and out stepped an aging black man, bearing a huge armload of wood. They froze in place. He was humming, seemingly oblivious to them, walking toward the house with his burden. Partway there, however, he suddenly dropped the wood and turned, facing them. In his hands was a sawed-off shotgun that had been hidden among the wood.

"All right there, sirs, you can just stay where you be," he said. "Who is it going there, and why?"

Bill said, "Jack? Heavenly days, is it you? Jack Field?"

The shotgun lowered a little. The old man squinted and cocked his head. "Who's that speaking to me?"

"Don't you recollect me, Jack? It's been many a year, but we've talked to one another time and again."

"Law! It's *you*! Ain't it? Is this here Mr. Bill Porterfield I'm talking to?"

"It's Porterfell, but I'll forgive the error, for it has been such a long time. It's good to see you, Jack. Why, I didn't even know you were still living!"

The shotgun was completely lowered now. The old man came close, hesitated, then put out a hand. He and Porterfell pumped arms mutually and vigorously.

"Jack," Porterfell said, "I want you to meet someone. This is my son, Kanati. Kanati, meet Jack Field, an old friend. He was a servant to Colonel Patrick back during the war."

There it was. Confirmation. The Proctor house indeed was occupied by people truly named Patrick. Why else would this man be here?

"Pleased to meet you," Kane said, shaking the old man's hand. "Thank you for not shooting us."

Jack Field looked puzzled. Adressing Porterfell, he said, "This is an Indian!"

"Only halfway," Porterfell said. "His mother was a Cherokee."

"I'll be!" Jack examined Kane as if he were a specimen of some rare bird.

"It's cold out here, Jack," Porterfell said, a none-too-subtle hint.

"Yes, yes it is," Jack said. "Let me get my wood up in arms here again, and I'll go to the house and talk to young Mr. Patrick."

"Did this Mr. Patrick come driving a wagon up here a little while ago?"

"Yes, sir, he did."

"I saw him. He looks like the colonel."

"Like the colonel used to, you mean. Years ago. Not like now."

"So he's alive? It's really true the colonel is still alive?"

Jack looked concerned. "I've said too much, sir. Seeing you here like this has made me careless. I can't say no more until I talk to young Mr. Patrick. He's young Mr. Proctor in the eyes of the world, of course. By the way, sir, what brings you up?"

"You might say I received a sort of invitation," Porterfell said.

Surprisingly, Jack seemed to comprehend at once what that meant and reacted with a somber nod.

"Ah, I see, sir. I see. You hold tight, sir, and I'll go talk to young Mr. Patrick."

The old servant labored up to a rear door with his load of wood, which he quickly stacked atop another pile beside the doorway. He was just reaching for the knob when the door opened, and the silhouetted form of the man in the wagon was revealed against the interior light.

Jack spoke to the man, glancing back at Kane and Porterfell, keeping his words low.

Kane shivered, anticipating an invitation inside, when instead the man in the door grabbed Jack's arm, yanked him in, and closed the door with a loud slam. There was a follow-up clatter of a latch being locked and a bar dropped in place.

Kane and Porterfell looked at one another. "We've made the wrong impression, I think," Porterfell said.

As obvious as it was that they were not welcome here, neither Kane nor his father gave a thought to trying to make it all the way back down to Helena. It was too cold, too snowy, too windy. They were near freezing where they were. They would never manage to trek all the way back to town without dire consequences.

So they headed for the woodshed from which Jack had emerged. It was cold inside, but at least the wind was cut by the thin walls. They could pass the night here, wait out the storm, and in this confined space use their mutual body heat to stay alive, if not comfortable.

"We're lucky they don't keep dogs," Kane commented.

"It's the dogs that are lucky," Porterfell countered. "If there were any handy, I'd roast and eat one of them. I'm starved."

Kane had put a little trail food into his pockets, just in case a snack was needed along the way, and now he shared this with his father. They were chewing and swallowing and shivering and dreading the long night ahead when they heard someone approaching the shed.

The door opened, revealing Jack, and just behind him the young man who was such a dead ringer for Colonel John Lindsey Patrick.

"Look, sir," Porterfell said, putting his hands out protectively. "We're only here because we knew we could never make it all the way back to—"

"No, no, never mind that," the young man said. "I apologize to you for shutting you out. When Jack told me your name was William Porterfell, I was so shocked that I reacted without thinking. Come inside, both of you. I have a big fire built, and you can warm yourselves."

"Obliged," said Porterfell. "Young man, I have to tell you: You are the very image of Colonel Patrick, under whose command I served in the late war."

"If I were talking to anyone else but a known member of Patrick's Raiders, as you are, Mr. Porterfell, I'd be telling you right now that any such resemblance is entirely coincidental, that my name is Proctor, and that I have never so much as heard of any Colonel Patrick. Given that you are who you are, though, I'll tell you quite honestly that the reason I resemble the colonel is that the colonel is my father."

"I'd thought as much. But he had no son before the war, meaning that . . ."

"That Colonel Patrick didn't die under sniper fire in Kentucky prior to the end of hostilities? Yes, sir, that's exactly true. He lived through it."

"Does he live still?"

"Come inside and see for yourself."

Chapter 25

The house was warm and well lit, an inviting reuge in the mounting blizzard. Kane and Bill Porterfell followed John "Proctor" Patrick into th
house . . .

. . . and immediately saw him.

He looked little like the pictures Kane had seen (
the dashing Silver Raider. Colonel John Lindsey Pa
rick, hiding here under the name of Proctor, looke
gray and old and stoop-shouldered, and the chair i
which he sat, with a blanket across his knees, was
wheelchair. Colonel Patrick seemed unaware that anone else was in the room with him. He was starin
into the fire, rocking, ever so slightly, back and fort
in his chair.

"How long has he been this way?" Bill Porterfe
asked in a funeral parlor whisper.

"To some measure, since the war. But he's ha
good years, too, in which he was almost strong an
lucid. I suppose my very existence is evidence of th
in that it takes a bit of clarity to go about sirin
children. It's only the last months that he's been lik
this . . . worse than ever, since Mother's death. He

declining fast. I don't anticipate he'll be much longer in this world, if he continues this way."

"May I speak to him?"

"Go ahead. But he won't hear you."

Bill Porterfell walked slowly over, circling around and kneeling slowly just to the colonel's side. He reached over and laid his hand on Patrick's arm.

"Colonel . . . it's good to see you. Do you remember me, sir? It's Bill Porterfell. It's been a lot of years, sir."

The colonel kept rocking and staring into the fire. It was as if Porterfell was not there.

Porterfell stared at his old leader for a long time, wiping away a tear. He patted Colonel Patrick's arm gently, stood, and walked back to join the others.

"I'd like to hear more about him," he said to John Patrick.

"Have a seat," Patrick said. "We'll talk."

"I have no knowledge of the war years, of course, having been born after that," John "Proctor" Patrick said, his hand wrapped around a mug of hot tea just provided for all of them by the silent and efficient Jack Field. "But I can tell you all I do know, and all I've been told.

"After Father was shot, he was believed to be dead, but a local farmer found him, alive, and took him to his home. In ways I've never fully had explained to me, word reached my mother of what had happened. She went to Father, found him hovering between life and death. And she brought him home secretly, keeping alive the official report that he had been killed.

"I'll belabor no details. Suffice it to say that Father was treated, pulled back from the edge of the grave. But he was, of course, not as he had been. The wounding had hurt him physically, and mentally. But Mother was true to him, fiercely protective. And determined that no one would know the shameful state that the proud Colonel John Lindsey Patrick, the Silver Raider, now existed in. She chose the name of Proctor for our family, and Proctor we became, though she shared with me and my sister, God rest her, the truth of who we were. We were instructed as to how important it was to keep our identities secret. And we did, faithfully, though it was hard for me as a boy not to want to brag to my friends about who I was, and who my father was . . . not the broken-down man they saw, but proud Colonel Patrick! The bravest raider of the Confederacy!"

"And so he was," Bill Porterfell said softly. "And so he was."

"Amen, and thank you. In any case, our family moved, here and there. Always Proctors before the public, but always Patricks at home, and proudly so. Mother had money, an inheritance, and we never lacked for what we needed. We lived in Texas, then Kansas, then Missouri, then Texas again, and at last came here.

"All this while, you must know, my mother was changing. Perhaps it was the difficulties of caring for a man in my father's condition, of bearing secrets forever, of going by a false surname . . . of always being afraid that we would somehow be found out, and the proud image of the dashing Colonel Patrick would be sullied by the much more ugly reality of what he'd become. In any event, Mother grew hateful and cold, and the worst of her anger she directed toward Patrick's Raiders. My father's own men. Especially his elite, central group . . . you, Robert Blessed, Jason Wyrick, Mack Brennan, Caleb Smith, Morton Rickerton, all of you. She blamed you, you see, for the shooting of my father. She swore that in one of his more lucid times, he told her he'd been shot not by Yankee snipers but by some of his own men."

Kane glanced at his father, recalling that Porterfell had told him his belief that Blessed and Wyrick had shot their own commander and wondering if he would confirm this with young Patrick. But Porterfell held his peace.

"As the years went by, her obsession with this idea grew and took hold of her. She talked about it, about the Punjab Star legend that had gotten so entwined with the Crosslin's Station incidents, and she sat up nights brooding, thinking about vengeance. It was a creeping mental deterioration, I can see now, but at the time I hardly knew what to make of it.

"I didn't know how far she'd taken her bitterness until recent months. I met a man, a detective for hire, who told me she'd hired him as her personal agent. She'd given him the task of tracking down the whereabouts of every member of the central core of Patrick's Raiders that he could and finding out how to reach them by mail. Then she'd written letters—the

agent never saw their contents—and paid him again
to travel from city to city, mailing these letters one
by one as he went. He never understood why he'd
been given this task, for it seemed insane to him . . .
but when he later learned that some of the recipients
of these letters had come to bad ends soon after they
would have received them and found out as well
that someone else had hired agents to find these
men—those agents no doubt being the instruments
of the murders—he grew worried about his part in
Mother's scheme. He came to me and confided what
had happened.

"I went through Mother's papers when she didn't
realize it and found copies of the letters. Written in
code—double coded, in fact. The old code of Patrick's
Raiders. And when put together and interpreted,
they directed the recipients to this very place and
implied that here the lost Punjab Star could be found.
She'd done a masterful job with those letters, placing
in each one of them enough information and hints to
make sure that each recipient could get a notion of
what was being hinted at. Each letter was designed
to stir the greed and the money lust of whoever was
able to interpret it. And she included in each the hint
that there were other letters, sent to other Raiders of
my father's inner circle, and that these letters contained the final pieces of the puzzle. It was brilliant,
in a diabolical, insane sort of way.

"I confronted her about it, of course. Her reaction
amazed me. She raged and spat and cursed, talking
of how much she hated Patrick's Raiders for what
they'd done to Father. She'd show them! She would

turn their wickedness inward, make them devour
one another! That was her plan, you see. She believed
that the old Raiders would all decide that missing
diamond might not be missing after all and would
begin stalking one another, trying to get those letters.
In her vision, she saw the Raiders destroying one
another in their lust for the diamond. Astonishing.
Absolutely astonishing . . . and absolutely mad." He
paused and sipped his tea.

"Perhaps it wasn't as mad as you think," Porterfell
said. "What she envisioned happened. Not with all
the Raiders. Just with two of them. Blessed and Wyrick. It was them who had the other Raiders killed
and their letters stolen. They got their hands on all
the letters but one—mine. They tried hard to get it,
even had me briefly kidnapped, but I escaped them.
Then they played another hand. They kidnapped Kanati, here, to hold him for bait, to lure me, to make
me surrender the final letter." Porterfell, helped and
sometimes corrected in details by Kane, outlined in
brief the ordeal that Kane had suffered, and his own
search for the truth, and how they'd only now come
together here in Helena, meeting for the first time in
their lives.

John Patrick was appropriately amazed. He ques-
tioned them, growing ever more appalled, for he
hadn't known until now that his mother's wild
scheme of vengeance had worked much more effi-
ciently than he could have ever imagined.

"I'm . . . *shocked*," Patrick said. "I had no idea that
such a thing had happened. Good Lord . . . I'd assumed that most of those who received the letters

would have simply thrown them away or kept them as a mystery to puzzle over. To think that anyone took them seriously, really believed there was a diamond to be had—"

Jack Field, silent in the corner, cocked his head and looked toward the door. Without a word or whisper of noise he rose, frowning, listening, and went to the doorway. He opened it, peered out as if looking for something or someone. A moment later he exited. He did all this so quietly that the others were hardly aware it had happened, except for the cold breeze that swept the room during the moments the door was open.

"I believe there was a diamond at Crosslin's Station," Porterfell said. "I even believe I know who wound up with it."

John Patrick looked quite skeptical. "Pardon my doubtfulness, sir, but I've never been able to convince myself that story has any truth in it. If there was a diamond there, either it would have been found later or it would have turned up purchased by some collector on the underground market. Neither of those things has happened. There could have been no diamond."

Porterfell frowned and found no answer to those points.

"I hope there is no diamond," Kane said. "It would be the proper justice for Robert Blessed to come this far only to find there was never anything to be had."

"My impression has always been that Blessed is a

bad man," Patrick said. "But to think he would go as far as what you've just described—"

"He's a desperate man," Kane said. "He had wealth, criminally gained, but is now on the brink of losing it all. He sees the Punjab Star as his only hope for survival."

"Where is he now? Did you tell me you've encountered him right here in Helena?"

"Yes."

Patrick stood up, frowning, and paced around a little. "Gentlemen, don't take this wrong, but hearing that makes me wish you hadn't come up here tonight."

"Perhaps we shouldn't have," Porterfell said. "But the impulse to know the truth was very strong. Now we do know. And now we should go, before we bring trouble to your door."

Ironically enough, it was just then that the door opened, and Jack Field entered the room, walking in clumsy fashion with an arm wrapped around his neck from behind, a pistol shoved against his temple, and the wide, glowering face of Robert Blessed looking across his shoulder.

John Patrick froze a moment, then reached for a rifle above the mantel. Bill Porterfell came to his feet, his hand groping toward his pistol. Kane simply rose and stared, feeling like the world's greatest betrayer and fool for having, along with his father, been unthinking enough to lead Blessed up here.

"I don't think I'd do anything rash, unless you want this boy's brains spread across this room,"

Blessed said. He eyed John Patrick. "Good Lord above, if it don't appear to be the very colonel himself, all young again! Don't tell me . . . a son? The old boy lived through it, did he, and had a son?"

"You're Robert Blessed," Patrick said, both a question and a statement.

"Indeed. And though I don't know precisely what's going on here, I do know that our two Porterfells there wouldn't have made a journey to such a place as this, in this kind of snow, without strong reason. Damnation! Is that Colonel Patrick I see in that wheeled chair?"

"It's a better man than you that you see, you scoundrel!" John Patrick said. "How dare you burst into my home, threaten my servant . . ."

"Enough words. I'm here for the diamond. I want it. Now."

"There is no diamond," Bill Porterfell said. "How's that for irony, Blessed? You've come this far, chased me, chased Kane, and murdered a woman I cared about, all for nothing."

"Oh, is that right? Well, blast. I may as well go home, then." Suddenly Blessed snarled and jammed the pistol so hard against the servant's temple that it made a round indentation. "Don't throw that bilge at me, Porterfell, especially about your 'love' for the half-breed's mother. You'd not have abandoned her if you loved her. And you'd not have come this far and run this hard and climbed this cursed mountain road in a snowstorm for a diamond that doesn't exist, nor united with a half-breed son you never even acknowledged if you didn't believe he could lead you to something valuable. You're no saint, not even a family man. So where is the diamond? I want it, or I start killing . . . first this darky, then that mindless stringbean in the wheelchair, then the rest of you. Talk!"

John Patrick looked quite pale. He licked his lips and began to tremble. "I have no choice," he said. "I have to tell the truth. There *is* a diamond."

Kane and Bill Porterfell stared at Patrick, astonished. Had the man lied to them? Or was he lying to Blessed?

"Aha! I knew it!" Blessed said. "Out with it, then! Hand it over!"

"It's not here," Patrick said. "It's out there. In the mountains."

"Hidden?"

"Yes. Well hidden. But simple to find if you know where it is."

"Then speak up! How do I reach it?"

"There's a cave, a hidden entrance . . ."

"A map. I'll have a map from you, sir. Sit down at that table. And draw. And waste no time about it, or you're all dead men."

John Patrick's hand trembled as he wrote and drew, and he glanced continually from his paper to the gun in Blessed's hand. Blessed, meanwhile, had Kane tie up Bill Porterfell, then had Jack Field tie up Kane, and then he tied up Jack Field himself.

John Patrick stood, handing the paper to Blessed.

"Here . . . take the cursed thing. Go away and

fetch your diamond—and may it drive you mad like it drives mad everyone who owns it!"

"Ah, the old curse story!" Blessed said, snatching the map. "Tell you what, sir, I'm not much for curse tales. The only curse I fear is that of poverty . . . but when that diamond is mine, there'll be no more of that, no, sir!" He studied the map closely. "Why the hell did you do nothing but hide that diamond in a cave? Why didn't you sell it? Make yourself rich?"

"Partly because it was our heritage, our savings, our future, if somehow we lost everything else. But the truth is, Blessed, that I hate the diamond. It's a wicked thing. It's brought nothing but despair to my family. So it's hidden away, never touched, never seen. Go! Find it and take it. I have no desire for it."

"So it was *you* who wrote the letters!"

"No. It was my mother. Dead and gone now. One of the last acts of her life. She wanted it found, wanted it taken . . . and hoped that in the taking of it, its thief would take the curse of it as well."

Blessed eyed the young man, then the colonel in his wheelchair, then the map, and shook his head. "There are stories here to be heard, I can see, but I've no time to hear them. I'm off, gentlemen. And so are you. Young sir, seat yourself in that chair and clasp your hands behind you."

"What will you do?"

"I'll tie you up, that's what. After that, I'll think a while. Try to decide how best to deal with you all."

Five minutes later, John Patrick was thoroughly trussed in his chair. Robert Blessed stood smiling triumphantly at the group of prisoners, then walked over and stared down at the listless, unaware Colonel Patrick.

After a few moments he shook his head. "If I'd known I was going to leave you like that, Colonel, I'd have taken a little better care when I shot you. Worse than being dead, I suppose, sitting there like a blob of dung. Well, not to worry. You'll be dead enough before long."

"What are you going to do, Blessed?" Kane demanded.

"I'm going to burn this house down around your ears, that's what. Then I'm going to march off into that blizzard out there and head for the mountains— and my diamond."

"You'll go out in this storm, in the dark?"

"Damned right. If I followed you up here, somebody else might have, too. I'll take no chances. I want that diamond as quick as I can put my hands on it."

"You'll freeze to death out there. And you'll never find a cave in the darkness, in terrain you don't know."

"If you're trying to buy yourself time, it isn't going to work. And I will find that cave. You forget, Kane, I was one of the best of Patrick's Raiders. I've tracked men in the mountains by night, found trails where no one else could. I'll have that diamond in my hands before morning . . . and by morning, all of you will be pieces of charred meat in a burned-out house that—too bad!—no one could reach to extinguish in time because of the storm."

"You're a madman, Blessed."

"Better a madman than a dead one." He smiled

cordially, and took a bottle of lamp oil from a shelf. He began spreading it around the room, soaking the floor, the furniture, the curtains. When he was finished, he threw the empty bottle into the fireplace, where it shattered. The residue of lamp oil inside it made the fire flare brightly. Colonel Patrick actually reacted, backing away from the flame . . . and as Kane watched, it seemed he turned his head, just a little, as if listening.

"It's been a pleasure, gentlemen," Blessed said. He pulled a cigar from his pocket, bit off the end, and thumbed a match aflame. He lit the cigar, puffed it a few times, got the coal glowing red. "See you in hell, my friends . . . but don't look for me anytime soon."

He touched the cigar to the oil-soaked sofa and watched the flames rise and spread. Smiling with satisfaction, he thrust the cigar back into his mouth, waved, and was forever gone.

Chapter 26

Heat and smoke, air too poisonous to breathe, bonds too tight to loosen. They all struggled frantically, but no one could get free. The fire was spreading incredibly fast. There was no hope that anyone would come, for there were no neighbors, and in this driving storm no firefighters from the town could hope to reach the house in time to save it or its occupants.

Kane knew they were going to die here. He pulled at his ropes until his wrists tore and bled, but he could not slip the bonds. He was growing weak, choking . . .

The smoke stung his eyes, blinding him.

"Bill!" he called. "Bill . . . can you hear me?"

He heard deep, painful coughing, someone seemingly trying to speak, but overcome.

"Pull on your bonds!" Kane yelled into the swirling, hot gray, quickly going orange as rising flames began to backlight the smoke. "Someone has to get free! If one of us can get free, he can free the others . . ." Kane's voice cut off, his mouth, nose, and lungs filling with smoke.

"Kanati!" It was Bill Porterfell's voice, weak and

strained. "Kanati . . . are you alive? Son, are you alive?"

Son. Even in the terror of the moment, Kane noticed the word. It was the first time Porterfell had called him that.

"I'm alive . . . Father. But it's hot . . . I can't breathe . . ."

John Patrick spoke. "Somebody's outside . . ."

At that moment the air grew suddenly hotter, the smoke shifting, the light of flames growing brighter . . . and the front door opened. Kane twisted his head and saw smoke swirling toward the open door and a figure stepping backward, struck in the face by it. But a moment later the figure drew closer again, peering into the smoke, recoiling a little at each gust of heat, but not running away.

A familiar figure . . . and Kane realized that someone besides Blessed had followed him and his father to this place.

"Spence!" Kane called. "Spence . . . you've got to help us!"

"That you, Kane?" Spence called. "How the hell did you get into this kind of a mess?"

"No time . . . to talk. Get us out, Spence!"

"Who all is in there?"

"Me, my father . . . and two others."

"Where's that Blessed fellow? I followed him up here."

"He's gone. He's the one who left us in this shape. Have mercy, Spence! Don't let us die in here! You've got to help us!"

"Maybe I will, maybe I won't. Depends on the diamond."

"You get us out, we'll help you find it."

"Where is it? You got it in there?"

Kane's mind raced. Now might be the worst time for truth. If Spence learned that the diamond was outside, that Blessed had gone after it, he might well leave them where they were, to their fate. Better to let him believe that the diamond could be his only if he spared them.

But circumstances intervened against Kane. John Patrick, full of terror for his father as well as himself, spoke up before Kane could.

"There is no diamond!" he said, his phrases punctuated by coughs, but his voice stronger than before by sheer force of will—and hope. "Sir, whoever you are, please save us. My father is here—he's old and crippled and feeble of mind!"

"No diamond? Then where's Blessed? Where'd he go?"

"He went after the diamond," John Patrick replied, panicking and doing quite a poor job of an extremely important and high-stakes conversation. "He's the one who did this to us! Please . . . *please* . . ."

"Aha! So there *is* a diamond!"

"No . . . no, I lied to him, trying to make him leave. I didn't know he'd try to kill us. Please, sir, my father is dying!"

"So Blessed is gone after the diamond! Then I'll be going after Blessed. I owe him one, anyway. The bastard tried to kill me, and almost did. Ought not be too hard to track him in the snow. I'll make me a torch—got any fire you can spare me?" He laughed heartily.

"For the love of God, sir, don't leave us!"

Kane chimed in. "Spence, you can't do this! You're a better man than this!"

"Nice of you to say, Kane, but talking time is through. My only interest in you was that diamond. And now you ain't got it. Fare thee well, gents! I'm off to track Mr. Blessed!"

"Dear Lord, Spence, don't do this!" Kane shouted.

"It's done, boys," Spence replied, backing away from the door, gleeful in his cruelty. "My mama always did tell me I was bound to turn out sorry. I suppose she was right!"

"In that case, there's no cause to leave you cluttering up the world any longer," a raspy voice behind him in the yard said. It was a voice Spence had heard before.

He whirled. A woman was approaching, the bottom of her skirts sticking out from beneath a heavy coat, trailing through the snow. In her hand was a revolver.

"Who the hell are you?" Spence asked.

"Remember Smithtown?" the woman replied.

Spence was silent for a moment then, "No . . . no, it ain't you. It ain't you."

"It is."

Spence cursed and went for his pistol.

The shots came fast, four in a row, so quickly fired they almost blended into one extended explosion. Two slugs ripped through Spence's stomach, another through his right lung, the last through his heart. He staggered back, through the doorway, and collapsed dead inside the hell of the burning house.

Outside, the Buckskin Belle slid her hot pistol into its holster beneath her coat, pulled a knife from her pocket, and walked into the house as if oblivious to the heat. She stepped over the corpse of Spence.

"Hello, gentlemen," she said. "If you'll hold tight, I'll have you cut free in just a few moments."

They made it out just as the flame and smoke became too much to take. They moved away from the house as quickly as they could—John Patrick carrying his father like a child, Kane and Porterfell walking arm in arm, leaning on one another, a father and son now, not just freshly acquainted strangers.

Jack Field stood to the side, looking at the flames engulfing the house. The blizzard, meanwhile, howled around them.

"It's gone, sir," Jack said.

"Yes," John Patrick said. "I don't think there'll be anything left."

"I'm sorry," Kane said. "It's our fault. We didn't realize Blessed was following us."

"You had a whole parade following you, it seems." He turned to Trudy. "I'm immensely grateful to you, ma'am. You saved our lives."

Trudy shrugged. "Ain't much of a thing, I don't reckon. I couldn't let nothing happen to Kane. Been following him, on the sneak, ever since we parted ways."

"You've been here all along?" Kane asked.

"I never did leave Helena, Kane. I know I was

supposed to . . . but durn it all, I felt you needed someone watching over you. And I did, whenever I could keep up with you. But you gave me the slip a few times.''

"You should have told me, should have showed yourself.''

"I almost did. Went right to your room door, then got scared and run when you came out.''

"So that was *you*! Scared? Scared of what?''

"Scared of . . . I don't know.'' She ducked her head. "Scared of maybe being more fond of you than I should be.''

Kane blinked, a little unsettled. "Trudy . . . I'm flattered. But there's already a woman. Waiting for me in Colorado.''

"I know. I didn't figure otherwise. But I hope that for the time that there was here . . . you and me riding together and all, that you found a friend to remember in Trudy O'Breen.''

Kane smiled at her. "Yes. A friend and a protector.''

"I'm glad you found your pap.''

"Yes. Come and meet him. And Trudy . . . you look quite lovely.''

"Hell,'' she said, tugging at the dress. "I hate the cussed thing. But I couldn't go around in buckskins, not after that Buckskin Belle nonsense come out in the paper. I put on my buckskins and I've got every fool young gun in the country after me.''

Trudy turned to John Patrick again. He was kneeling now, arm around his father, who was wrapped in some horse blankets Jack Field had found. "I'm sorry your house burned," she said.

"The devil take it," John Patrick said. "It's only a house."

"I feel like it's my fault," Kane said again.

"It wasn't your fault, Mr. Porterfell. What caught up with us tonight was the past. It always does, they tell me."

"We're going to get cold out here, sir," Jack said. "I suggest we move to the barn."

"I have to know something," Kane asked, once they'd settled into the barn and started a fire in the center of the dirt floor. "Is there really a diamond?"

"There is . . . but not of the sort that Mr. Blessed thinks he'll find," John Patrick replied.

"What do you mean?" Kane asked.

"Wait until day. Wait until the clouds are gone. Then look at the mountains and see."

No matter how they pressed him, that was all that John Patrick would say.

The blizzard was the worst the mountain country had seen in years. Snow, driven in the wind, fell without ceasing. For three days all commerce and travel ceased.

The blizzard finally ceased, though the clouds remained. The railroad men went to work clearing the tracks, merchants and civil servants and volunteers with big shovels went to work clearing the streets and boardwalks, and the trains ran again. By now Kane and Bill Porterfell had said their good-byes to the Patricks, who had withdrawn into the protection of their Proctor pseudonym and had taken up rooms in the best hotel in town, already making building plans for the spring. Stanley Kriger had come around, begging for information, begging for a story, begging to know all about the Punjab Star, and in the end, begging all for nothing, because they declined to tell him a thing. This episode of life was through, and they had no desire to rehash it. And they had every desire to get out of Helena before the rubble of the Proctor house was searched, and the burned remains of Spence were found.

Kane and Bill Porterfell knew where they were going. In the mining town of Three Mile, Colorado, Carolina Railey waited for Kane, and he was eager to see her again. And this time, he would have his father at his side.

Kane was alone no more. He had no diamond, but it didn't matter. His treasure was in the person of the man at his side and the beautiful young woman who soon would be, again.

The sun came out the day that Kane and Bill Porterfell prepared to catch the eastbound train and leave Helena behind. Kane paused on the street, looking around at the town, the mountains beyond.

"It's beautiful," he said. "The snow sparkles in the sun like . . ."

"Go ahead and say it. Like diamonds."

Kane looked at the peaks in the distance. "Do you think Blessed found what he was looking for?"

"I doubt it. From what young Mr. Patrick said, his talk about the Punjab Star was a ruse. I never did come to understand what he meant about there being a diamond in the mountains, but not the one Blessed wanted."

"Blessed died out there," Kane said. "How could anyone have lived through that storm? And the fool plunged into it at night!"

"Because he had to. He had to dispose of us and get his little show moving down the road while there was darkness and storm to cover his tracks. But I suspect you're right. I suspect the wilderness has claimed Robert Blessed for good."

"And good riddance if it has."

"Amen, Kane. Amen."

They continued walking, toward the train station.

Trudy O'Breen was waiting when they got there. It had taken Kane a lot of persuading to get her to agree to come with them to Colorado. When finally she relented, though, she did so enthusiastically. In Colorado there would be new opportunities, she said. In the town of Three Mile there would be no Buckskin Belle, no gunslingers in her shadow. She could start a new way of life. Maybe mine a little.

"Kanati," Bill Porterfell said as the train circled around and headed out of town. "Look." He pointed out the window toward the mountains.

Shining in the sun, reflecting it back in brilliant splendor, was a gleaming stone surface on the mountainside. Though it looked small from this distance, Kane figured it must be scores of feet across, and the same again vertically. A mineral deposit of some sort, he figured . . . but when the light struck it right, it shone with the brilliance, and roughly the outline, of a great cut diamond.

"There it is," Bill Porterfell said. "There's what young Mr. Patrick was talking of. There's the diamond that Mrs. Patrick saw gleaming down at her from the mountainside, putting into her head, over time, the idea of using the Punjab Star tale to take her vengeance on the men she blamed for the ruination of her husband. That's it. That's the thing that started it all."

"You believe so?"

"Let's say I strongly suspect so."

Kane looked at the gleaming diamond light on the mountain until the train's angle changed sufficiently to alter the angle at which he saw it. Then the "diamond" vanished forever from his view.

He did not look back again. The chase was over. He was alive and no longer alone, and the future shone bright, brighter than any jewel and richer by far.

Epilogue

Two seasons later, two stories appeared within one week's editions of the *Territorial Voice*, Helena, Montana Territory.

The first story gave a grim account of a skeleton being found by two hunters in the mountains. The skeleton was that of a large man, clad in heavy winter clothing, armed, and with a piece of paper clutched in his hand. Though weathering had obliterated most of the markings on it, it was thought to have once been a map.

The man was unidentified despite many efforts, and his remains lay now in an unmarked pauper's grave. He was dismissed as a casualty of the year's heavy January blizzards, and forgotten.

The second story, picked up from the Eastern newspapers and of particular interest to the *Voice*'s senior reporter, Stanley Kriger, concerned the unexpected discovery of a long-lost jewel, the legendary Punjab Star, in an unexpected place: inside the wall of a New York tenement house.

The great blue jewel had been stashed in the wall of a room that had been occupied for many years by a former Southerner named Maxwell "Mack" Brennan, a seldom-employed vagrant whom neighbors had long believed insane. How he had managed to come by the stone no one knew, though some said that Brennan had claimed at times to have ridden with Patrick's Raiders, the famed rebel band whose legend intertwined with that of the Punjab Star.

Brennan had died penniless, having never converted the inestimably valuable jewel to cash. As Brennan had no heirs, his jewel had reverted to the state, and debate was strong, the newspaper reported, over what should be done with it.

Two weeks later, the *Voice* carried a tiny notice of a marriage in Colorado between one Kane Porterfell, "a former visitor to Helena," and Carolina Railey, daughter of a traveling showman.

Stanley Kriger was responsible for running that notice, though he knew it would mean little to anyone in Helena. But Kane and his wife had gone to the trouble of sending him the information, so he had it published. He clipped out a copy from the first run of that day's paper and tacked it to his wall.

He sent the bride, whom he'd never met, a present. It wasn't much, just a cheap necklace of blue glass cut in the shape of a diamond and placed in an inexpensive setting. But it was the best Kriger could afford, and all in all, he suspected Kane and his wife would find it symbolically a most appropriate gift.